THE REDNECK POACHER'S SON

A novel by Luke Wallin

The Redneck Poacher's Son

Bradbury Press   Scarsdale   New York

Library of Congress Cataloging in Publication Data
Wallin, Luke. The redneck poacher's son.
Summary: The youngest of three sons raised to be poachers in the Alabama
swamps rises above the snare of his destiny.
  I. Title
PZ7.W15934Re   [Fic]   80-26782
ISBN 0-02-792480-7

For my Father and Mother
Luther Wallin, Jr., Ruth McMullan Wallin

My Children
Smoke, Clay, Rain

And for Mary

THE REDNECK
POACHER'S SON

PART I

In the Swamp

Chapter 1

Jesse Watersmith walked through the clearing with his father.

"Boy," Paw said, "you doin mighty good."

He put one long arm around his son's shoulders and squeezed him.

"Thanks," Jesse said. "I don't have long, you know."

"Before the hot weather?"

"Yes, sir. This spring has been so cool—it's the latest we've ever been able to trap."

"You right about that."

Paw swung the whiskey bottle in his free hand. "I hate to see the heat," he said.

"I know you do."

Paw stopped walking and Jesse waited while he raised the bottle to the sky and took a long drink. "You grab a fox or a cat one day," he said, "shake his hair, and it's tight as the hair on your head. You know that?"

"I know it."

"Next day, sun's been workin on him a little more, and that fur comes off like feathers."

"Yes, sir. Aunt May says the Lord does it to stop trapping."

"She said that?" Paw's thin lips twisted angrily. Then he relaxed and smiled, with a slightly hurt look in his eyes. "Who knows, Jesse? Maybe it's the truth. I just hope one thing, son. I hope you catch me a good bobcat before it's too late. Think you can do that?"

Jesse smiled, trying to act relaxed. I might catch you one more fox, he thought, but not a cat. Not a bobcat as long as I have anything to do with it.

"I'm countin on you," Paw said with a wink.

The bobcat was the only animal Jesse refused to trap. He couldn't tell Paw or his brothers, not just because they would laugh at him, but also because Paw would beat him if he found out. Jesse checked all the traps faithfully and brought in foxes and raccoons, opossums and skunks for Paw to sell. But he watched all the time for bobcat tracks, and when they were fresh on his trapline trails, he always moved his sets.

Paw drank again. Jesse watched the clear moonshine trickle down his chin. "Where's your aunt, anyway?" Paw asked.

"Gone to town with Robert Elmer."

"Oh?" Suddenly Paw looked agitated. "I *know* you seen that cat," he said.

"Sir?"

"You had to. Ain't you seen it?"

"I . . . I never did."

"You spent so much time in the woods, and you done so good catchin things."

"But I never caught a cat."

"I know you didn't, son. That's the problem, ain't it?"

Jesse looked into the trees.

"Now, let me tell you somethin, and I don't want you to forget it."

Jesse waited. His father's arm felt like a log on his shoulders.

"I can get a hundred dollars for a catskin now. Price might not hold, but that's what I can get to-day."

Jesse was shocked: a good fox only brought forty-five.

"But the season's over!" Jesse said. "You can't sell it until next fall, and by then—"

"By then the price might be down? I know that. Don't you think I know that? But it might not, too. It sho might not."

"Well, I just haven't—"

"Ain't you?"

The fire came in Paw's watery light blue eyes. His stare jumped back and forth, like it always did when he was nervous.

"No, sir! I haven't seen any tracks! I don't know where that bobcat went!"

"I bet you don't!" Paw yelled. His words slurred together. "You the best trapper I ever seen, Jesse. I taught you the whole works, and you better than me. So just don't tell me you don't know!"

Paw's eyes were switching.

"I'll get you one if I can," Jesse said desperately, "honest I will."

"Honest? Honest?"

The eyes jumped like the tail of a cat, before he strikes.

"Yes, sir, I will, I'll get you one."

Paw's face was red, his beard stubble white-gray. The rivers in his forehead were folded deep.

"You better get me the one you seen, boy."

"But—"

"Shut up! I checked your traps myself yesterday, just to see. And you know what I found? I found fresh tracks on the sage hill trail. Fresh tracks there, and no traps at all!"

"I didn't see them!"

"You get some traps out there, Jesse. Get em out this afternoon. Don't you fool with Twaint Watersmith. I want that cat this week."

"Yes, sir, I will."

"Don't you lie to me. Don't you ever lie to your Paw."

"I'm not!" Jesse walked away from him.

"Hold on! Where you headed?"

"I'm gonna set out the traps for you."

"Wait a minute."

Jesse stood there, breathing hard.

"I want you to come with me first."

"Come where?"

"You'll see."

Paw grinned. It was a crazy, drunken grin, but it was also like a kid's. He danced past Jesse as if he had forgotten yelling at him, went into his sagging trailer and came out with a big bottle of blue shaving lotion. "Hold this," he said.

Jesse took it.

Paw winked at him, as if they were in on a secret together.

Then Jesse followed his father out of their clearing, off into the spring swamp. The tender new leaves were out, thin and light green, but they could still see a long way.

Soon Jesse realized they were headed for the whiskey still hidden in the pine thicket.

Paw stopped and looked back at him, grinning as if they were buddies. Then he took a long pull on the bottle. Jesse's heart was still beating hard. How can he act like nothing happened? he thought.

Jesse knew he had to get away soon. He was getting too old to let Paw treat him this way, and he was afraid of what was coming. Lately Paw was drinking more and more.

They came to a stretch of the trail where leaves were blown away and bare mud was exposed. Jesse watched carefully as they walked along: raccoon prints, squirrel, the twisted groove of an early snake . . . and cat tracks! Jesse stepped on them, mashing them down in the soft ground, trying to get every one. Paw hadn't noticed.

The pines appeared through the trees.

Paw stopped, put a bony finger to his lips, and they listened.

The woods were quiet, just a mockingbird fussing far away.

They crept softly through the sweet-smelling

pines, and after a hundred yards came to the moon-shine still.

They had finished making a big run last week, and the boiler, vats, cooling barrel, and mash boxes all stood strangely quiet. Jesse thought of having worked two days and nights straight, alongside Paw and his older brothers, Robert Elmer and Bean. Now the three white oak barrels on the edge of the honey-suckle held their precious whiskey, a little more than a hundred gallons.

Paw moved through his still, touching each piece lightly as he passed. When he came to the barrels, he turned around and looked at Jesse.

"Two of these are all right," he said. "But this last one was made with Robert Elmer in charge of the fire."

Jesse waited.

"Robert Elmer *said* he could stay awake."

"We'd been up for two whole nights, Paw."

"Don't you tell me! He'd been up longer than that, chasin that woman in town. Anyway, you know what he done?"

"Let it scorch?"

"How'd you know that?"

"I just guessed."

"You ain't tasted it?"

"Paw, you know I never tasted whiskey in my life, except what Aunt May gave me for the cough."

"Well, he let it scorch all right. He fell to sleep on the ground by the fire. That boy comes in like a hound runnin coon three days, says he's ready for work, lays on the dirt and passes out. Don't that beat all?"

"Yes, sir."

"Don't it?" Paw was grinning.

"Yes, sir." Jesse smiled a little.

Paw started to laugh. He seemed proud of Robert Elmer.

"That brother of yours! He lives just like a dog on the loose! Comes in here . . ."

Now they were laughing together. Jesse couldn't help it.

"Ain't it the truth?"

"Yes, Paw, it's the truth."

Paw cackled and cackled and slowly stopped laughing.

"Well, he fixed me good. I can't afford for every stitch of my still to be copper, now I just can't. And you got to watch that fire like it *meant* somethin to you! You know that?"

"Yes, Paw."

"All right then. It ain't all copper, and Robert Elmer ain't all what he's supposed to be, and so I got me a big old barrel of burnt tasting moonshine."

Jesse watched Paw take another long drink.

"Gimme that stuff."

Jesse handed him the bottle of shaving lotion.

Paw pried the cap off the wooden barrel and poured in the blue liquid.

"No, Paw!"

"Hush, boy."

He picked up a long whittled stick and poked it into the barrel.

As he stirred he grinned. "Them other barrels," he said, "go to the regular customers."

Paw chuckled in his throat, looking at his knotty hand turn the stick.

"And this barrel here, this will go to any strangers that show up wanting some."

Jesse felt sick.

When he was younger, and Paw in better shape, Jesse had learned to take pride in their whiskey. In those days the still *was* all copper, no matter what it cost. Suddenly it hit Jesse that what he'd heard might be true: Watersmith whiskey had killed two men.

When Paw finished and replaced the barrel cap, he motioned for Jesse to follow him.

They sat down in the midst of the quiet still.

"You know what I hate about the hot weather, Jesse?"

"No."

"It ain't the heat. I never did care one way or the other, for the heat or the cold. Reckon that's why I always lived outside."

"Yes, sir."

"It ain't the heat. It's my huntin, my deer. I killed nineteen this last year, son, nineteen."

"I know, I dressed them."

"And you sure did, too. Sure did."

Paw leaned back on his cooling barrel. He closed his eyes, and Jesse watched his face. It seemed harmless, roundish and pink, with blond eyebrows and a stubble of gray. The deep creases from eyes and mouth and across his brow relaxed a little. And his thin hair, half dirty blond and half gray, lifted gently in the breeze.

"Jesse, I dream about the deer every night. Did you know that?"

"Yes, sir, you've told me."

Paw opened one eye.

"Eh? Well, it's true." He closed it again. "Every night I watch them, down the barrel of my rifle. Big bucks, Jesse, *big* fat bucks. I kill them over and over again, a thousand times."

They sat there in silence a long while. Jesse had grown up with Paw and his brothers killing deer all the time, and he had learned to skin and quarter and butcher the meat long before he could reach the bodies hanging from the white oak tree in camp.

Jesse was sickened by the thought of killing deer, but he had never minded his job. Partly because he'd been doing it since before he could remember, and partly because every animal—the smell, touch, taste of them, inside and out—was sacred to him. He loved the animals with such a strong feeling that he would linger over them alive—touching a living wasp or a grinning, sharp-toothed raccoon—or dead, layer by layer, feeling skin and muscles and organs and the bones themselves. He loved feathers, old teeth of foxes found in the woods, hooves of fawns lying in blond piles of fur two months after a coyote had struck. So he never minded dressing the deer, just as he had never minded the trapline.

"But I cannot get to the bottom of the well," Paw said. "If I live a hundred years, I won't kill enough of em."

Paw opened his eyes.

Jesse nodded. He couldn't feel what Paw felt about this, but he'd heard it all his life.

"And it's a sin that a man like me can't have no land."

"Yes, sir."

Paw sat up straight and Jesse saw the anger darken his face.

"They call me a poacher, Jesse. A worthless poacher, a redneck poacher. They say my name and they spit. Well, I say the hell with them all. If they didn't have no land, where would they hunt? Tell me that?"

"You're right, Paw."

"Course I'm right. Wouldn't a damn one of them let me hunt on his land if I asked him, and I sho never would. I never would."

"I don't blame you."

"That's a good boy, son. Your Paw ain't no bad man. I was born into this world outside the law, and that's the way I'll die."

Paw took a slow drink of his whiskey.

It was noon. Jesse noticed the sun high through openings in the breezy pines. But it was shady in the thicket, and the sun was cool.

"You too, Jesse. Don't never trust them town people. They all think they're better than us; they'd love to see us slip and fall. But I'll tell you one thing . . ."

He smiled, looking satisfied, at his bottle.

"They're as scared of me as they can get. You let any of them landowners come upon me in his woods, and all I got to do is look him square in the eye and say, 'So sorry, Mister, reckon I'm lost.' That's all I got to say, and they'll pretend like it's true."

He laughed and Jesse smiled with him.

"They don't know what would happen if they got smart with me. Now, they really don't."

Jesse couldn't help chuckling at his father's pleasure.

"And I'll tell you a secret, boy, I sho will: I don't know myself."

They sat quietly for a moment.

Jesse remembered sitting in the woods with Paw when he was younger, listening to him, learning about the animals and the whiskey making. He missed those times.

"You take the deer right on this ground where we're sittin. You know who they belong to?"

"Belong to?"

"That's right. When you crossed the creek back yonder you left Dr. Walker's land and stepped onto Mr. Will Evans' place. Know who he is?"

"I've heard you cuss him, Paw."

"That's right. Evans' Sawmill in town. You know now?"

"I've seen his mill."

"Well," Paw said, "I have worked in his damn mill. Used to pull lumber off the green chain, drive trucks, and guide the logging crew. You know your Paw did all that?"

"No."

"I sure did. I didn't mind it, neither. Evans said I was the best man with a chain saw he'd ever seen."

He smiled and took another swallow. "Then one day, out of the clear blue, he fired me. Didn't ask my side of it, didn't give me no chance. Just told me to get out of his sight."

His eyes narrowed and the lines spread out from them, and his forehead wrinkled up like beechbark. Paw looked down at the ground and spit.

"Paw," Jesse asked, "why did Mr. Evans fire you?"

"He said I burnt down a shack. Belonged to a black that worked for him called Nathan. Know him?"

"No."

"Well, I never did that. Leave it to old Nathan to burn his own house, and blame me."

They sat together in silence for a little while. Then Paw stretched and closed his eyes, and opened them again.

"I think I'll have me a nap now, son."

"All right."

"Jesse?" he said softly, in his throat.

"Sir?"

"Ain't you got something to do?"

"I told Aunt May I'd pick her some fresh cattails."

Paw's face turned a darker red and his eyes started their cat's twitch.

"Something else, I mean. You ain't forgot, have you?"

"No sir."

Jesse got to his feet.

"Good. Get to it. Get them traps out this afternoon."

"I will."

"You damn right you will. You catch me that bobcat by the end of the week or I'll whip you good. You sixteen now, and you gettin big, but that don't mean nothin to me."

Jesse turned and walked past the still into the pines.

When he was out of sight he started to run.

Chapter 2

He ran down the trail toward camp. Sharp wild plum branches scratched his face and arms but he didn't care. Every time it happened with Paw he promised himself to stop pretending he had a father. With every shock of his boot on the ground he thought of hitting him. Robert Elmer fought Paw once, when he got too old to take the whippings. Will I have to do that too? Jesse wondered.

He heard a crow screaming close by in the switch-cane. He stopped suddenly, breathing hard against a tree, and listened. He waited and another one came, then two more. Their sharp, grating voices matched his feelings; he crouched down and slipped toward them in the cane. He stopped under the cover of a hackberry tree that was wound tightly by a flowering wisteria vine. Motionless, he couldn't be seen from the air. He called three times, sharply, just enough to get their attention, and the crows waited. His anger at his father turned to anger at the smart-aleck crows. Finally one of them answered, but he didn't reply.

Another whole minute passed, and he heard the hard brush of wings and the swish of a landing in the tree high above him. The other crows started up loudly now, and dozens came flying from across the swamp. The sentry above never made a sound.

Time passed, and Jesse grew uncomfortable. He wanted to scratch his head. He wanted to get some lunch. The winey smell of wisteria was strong all around him. If he moved, the lookout would give alarm and they would all be gone, broadcasting the news of his presence over the woods. And, he thought, they'd be saying they got the better of me, they sure would.

Two minutes passed. Jesse's leg started to cramp. He was sorry he'd started it, but he wanted to prove something. Then the sentry crow flew down to the top of a sapling near him. In a moment of looking around, cocking its shiny black head this way and that, it spotted the bright skin of his face. Ayy! Ayy! Ayy! the crow cried, flapping hard up through the branches. The whole gang was off across the trees now, ringing their disdain and, Jesse hoped, their embarrassment.

It was a standoff, he thought. I didn't give in and I didn't make a mistake, and neither did they. I'll just have to get something to cover my face if I'm going to fool them.

Jesse set off for the pond to get Aunt May's cattails. The young stalks would be tender and tasty this time of year. He heard a fox squirrel fussing and barking nearby, and he stopped to listen.

His brother Bean came through the saplings.

Jesse whistled, their rising signal note, like a female quail.

"Ho!" Bean said, startled.

He grinned and came over.

Bean was twenty. He was six feet tall, with reddish blond hair, a long friendly face like a young hound, freckles and Paw's watery blue eyes. To Jesse, he looked like an older version of himself, except that Jesse's face was rounder, and his eyes were dark brown.

"What you doin, boy?" Bean asked in his quick, nasal voice.

"I'm going for cattails."

"At the little pond?"

"Yeah. Want to come?"

"All right. I've got about an hour, then I have to deliver some shine."

"Who to?"

They started walking together.

"Red Herrick's fish store."

"You know about the scorched barrel?"

"Yeah. Third one, ain't it?"

"Uh-huh."

"I'll leave that for Paw to dispose of."

"He poured shaving lotion in it."

Bean laughed. "Where'd he get it from?"

"That's a good question."

"Maybe he had it just for this."

"What would it do, Bean? If you drank it?"

"Shoot!" Bean said, smiling and spitting into the weeds. "I'd hate to find out!"

"That's horrible. Don't you think so?"

"Aw, I reckon."

"He used to teach us to be so careful with it."

"Yeah."

"Listen, Bean, did our whiskey ever kill anybody?"

"Who told you that?"

"Never mind. Did it?"

"I don't know."

"Tell me the truth."

"It made some people sick, that's all I heard." Bean looked away from Jesse.

They came to the pond. Jesse walked out on a spit of land. On either side were fresh young cattails. He began pulling them up and cutting off the dangling root tendrils and top leaves with his knife.

"You could help," he said gently to Bean.

"Oh, all right."

Bean poked among them, as if he wanted to find one that wouldn't get him muddy or wet. "You want to go seining with me this week?"

"Sure."

"Okay. Aunt May says if we get her a turtle, she'll cook up a good soup."

"Mmmm," Jesse said. "I remember the last one."

"Yeah. We need to do it right away. I was down at the beaver dam pond yesterday, and I saw about a twenty pound catfish roll."

"Boy, I'd sure like to get him."

"Yeah. Let's get Robert Elmer and go seining."

"Not today," Jesse said.

"Why not?"

"Paw might want to go with us and he's hitting his whiskey pretty hard. I left him asleep at the still."

"He was nasty?"

"Yeah."

"Glad you told me. I'll see if I can't pick up my shine for the delivery after he's gone."

Jesse felt good, sharing things with his brother. He remembered when he could trust Bean, and they spent time together. But in the last couple of years Bean had grown moody like Paw.

"Bean," Jesse said.

"What?"

They were walking back with the stalks.

"Do you think you'll stay in this swamp forever?"

"Forever?" Bean grinned and Jesse saw the spaces where two teeth were missing.

"You know what I mean."

"I don't know. Hell, you can't never tell what life will bring."

"Don't you ever want to get out? See what it's like?"

"Well, I do get out, at night, on the highway strip. Robert Elmer's got him a woman you wouldn't believe down there. I'll carry you with us sometime."

Jesse walked along in silence.

"I'll tell you one thing, though, little brother. If you tried to leave here, you'd have to go one hell of a long way. Because soon as folks hear your name is Watersmith, they figure you're no damn good."

"That's what Paw claims."

"You'll find out," Bean said, "and just a little taste of it will be enough."

As they walked into camp, they saw a fire catching up beneath the big washing cauldron. Aunt May came quickly out of Bean's tent with an armload of dirty clothes. She was heading into Jesse's tent when she saw them. "Well!" she cried. "Just what I need right now, two pairs of arms!"

They smiled and Jesse ran to take her bundle. "I'm all right!" she said, jerking it from him. "I'm not that weak! Just go gather up the rest of the stuff."

"Yes, ma'am," he said.

"Bean," she continued, "if you wouldn't mind, sir, how about splitting a little more wood and stacking it by the pot?"

"Might as well," he grumbled.

"Yes," she said sharply but softly, "if you want clean clothes you might."

Jesse collected all the shirts and jeans and overalls and even the damp cot sheets, and stuffed them down in the hot spring water. Then he brought the fresh chunks of white oak as they fell away from Bean's axe, and laid them neatly by the cauldron.

"Boys," Aunt May said, "come over here and listen to me a minute. I got news." She straightened up from stirring the wash, set her strong, taut arms in a country woman's stance, fists on hips, and surveyed the clearing. Her face was crosshatched with shallow wrinkles in the soft skin, and her brown eyes were as sad and careful as a deer's. Her right eye was almost back to normal, from where Paw had hit her two weeks ago; the purple and bluish skin had faded out to a greenish yellow.

"Reason I'm so late with my washing today—and y'all might have to sleep without sheets unless we get a good dry wind—is I been visitin in town with my friend Elmilly."

"How is that old woman?" Bean asked.

"Not too old to do you a big favor, young man."

"Huh?"

"That's right. She's an old friend of the Evans family in town, and I asked her to see what she could find out about jobs for you all down at the sawmill."

"Aunt May, that man hates Paw," Bean said.

"Just hold on, hold on. Mr. Evans is a good man. He might not be carrying the same kind of grudge as your Paw."

"Aw," Bean said, "I bet you—"

"Listen!" Aunt May said sharply. "Now, the word has come through, just today, that all three of you boys can try out at the mill, and he'll even take your Paw on with the woods crew."

"A job?" Jesse asked.

"How'd you like that?" his aunt said, smiling at him. "You'd live in town, work down there all summer. Just think of that."

"He'll never let us," Jesse said.

"Don't be so sure!" Aunt May said. "They're about ready to elect a sheriff in town. Now, does anybody remember what happened the last time they did that?"

They looked at each other and shook their heads.

"Think! Paw had to stop his whiskey business until it was over."

"Oh, yeah," Bean said. "Boy was he mad."

"Uh-huh. Well, if that happens again, all he'll have left is the deer meat trade, and he just *might* be glad to have some steady cash."

"I wouldn't mind," Bean said. "I could take that sawmill for a while."

"Mind?" Jesse said. "Shoot. I'd give anything to get out of here."

"That's what I thought," Aunt May said. "Now you just let me pick the right time to tell your paw, okay?"

"No argument on that," Bean said. "What about Robert Elmer?"

"He went to town with me," she said, "and he's all for it."

They heard a stick break at the far end of the clearing, and Paw walked unsteadily into view.

"Uh oh," Bean said, "time for me to make my whiskey run."

"Remember," Aunt May said, "let me tell him."

Bean winked and took off into the woods. Paw raised his arm as if he wanted to catch him, but couldn't think what to say. Then he leaned against his trailer.

Jesse walked over to him, bent down and pulled out some traps from under the steps. As he rose, Paw's arm came flying at his head, and he flinched and ducked. Paw staggered slightly and rested against Jesse's shoulders. "Here, son!" he said with a loose grin. "I just wanted to give you a little pat on the back."

"Oh."

"Sho! I didn't mean you no harm. Jeez, boy, you skittish as a rabbit."

"I'm going to set the cat traps now, Paw."

"Eh? You ain't done that yet?"

"I've been helping Aunt May."

"I bet. I just bet. You bout as reliable as Robert Elmer."

Jesse walked into the trees with the traps over his shoulder. His teeth were set tight, and he was grateful that Paw didn't yell after him.

So here I go, he thought bitterly, off to catch my cat. He had that feeling Paw had given him so many times before in his life, that the only way he could please the old man was by doing something he knew was wrong.

Chapter 3

He headed for the sage hill. Clouds were blowing in, lower and lower, and the air was getting warmer by the hour. It looked like a storm coming from the southwest.

As he walked along, he tried to imagine how he could set the traps and yet not catch the cat. Paw knew exactly where she traveled, all right.

He thought about the first time he'd seen her, three weeks ago. He had been high in the fork of a red oak, watching the trail where her tracks always disappeared into the sage hill thicket. Ten minutes before the last light of sundown, she had stepped out. Like an alert, living cloud of smoke, she had emerged from thick plum bushes, stood looking back and forth, and finally padded, soundlessly, into the sagegrass.

His heart was pounding, recalling it . . .

He knew he'd see her if he just waited there long enough. And he knew her den must be in the folds of that hill, completely thatched over with plum and briar and honeysuckle. Jesse thought about the bobcat, so different from all the other animals in the swamp, and wondered why she meant so much to him. He had loved trapping when he was a little boy, but with each passing year he'd come more and more to hate the animals' pain. It wasn't as if they had to trap for a living.

That night Paw came into his tent, waving the bottle and accusing him of knowing where a bobcat was. "How?" Jesse asked Aunt May. "How on earth could he have known?"

"Ain't much he misses, Jesse," she said. "You know you're kind of a give away about these bobcats."

He turned from her, embarrassed. He knew that when he was younger and Paw occasionally had trapped one and brought it in, he had stared at it with a wonder they had all noticed.

"I don't even understand it myself," he said to her.

She just looked at him.

"What's wrong with me, Aunt May? Do you think I'm silly to care about them?"

She patted him on the leg. "Not a thing wrong, Jesse. Let me ask you a question. Do you recall when we first moved here, from that old house on the highway?"

"No, ma'am."

"You were four. You don't remember that at all?"

"No." Jesse grew sad and looked away from her.

"It was soon after that when your mama died."

He turned, alert. Information about his mother was hard to get.

"She had a pet that year. Do you know what it was?"

He shook his head.

"Well, she was friendly with this logging foreman. He'd bring her animals from the trees they cut down. One time *he gave Bean a baby coon. That thing was more trouble than a rattlesnake."*

Jesse smiled.

"And he brought you a flying squirrel, but it didn't live. Jesse, the last time he ever came up here, last time your Paw would allow him to, he gave Tanya a wildcat kitten."

Jesse sat up on his cot.

"Now do you remember?"

He shook his head, searching a missing stretch of memory.

"She was eaten up with that thing, in a manner of saying. They had cut a big old beech tree in the spring, and this cat had hidden her kittens down in a hollow under the roots. The man just happened to look down, and saw it duck back in the hole."

"And he caught it?"

"With a pair of gloves. That little thing was mad! You should have seen it spit and scratch! Well, of course, you did."

"I did?"

"You were four, like I said. That kitty was your best friend."

"But I don't—"

"I know you don't remember. Ever since your mama's been gone, there's been no talk of her, nothing to remind you."

"She loved that cat?"

"Oh, yes. Lay in her hammock between the two poplar trees with it by the hour."

"And it got big?"

"Huge. Turned out to be a male. It killed a hound your Paw had. He wasn't too pleased about that."

"What ever happened to him? The cat."

"He, well like I say, he got so big . . . He just ran off one day. I reckon it was time. . . ."

Jesse tried to remember his mother's bobcat. It was no use. As he walked to the sage hill with the traps over his shoulder, he tried picturing her, too, the mother Aunt May had described. He did remember the day Paw said she had drowned . . .

"And no," he said, "you won't never see your mama no more, so don't start askin for her." Then Paw had taken him in his arms and hugged him. Jesse was trying to understand the words, and what they could really mean, when the loud strange sound of Paw's sobbing began. Paw held him a long time, until Jesse was scared . . .

Jesse reached the den thicket. Just as he expected, there was a fresh set of prints going into the honeysuckle.

He sat down on the ground and crossed his legs. The wind was picking up and a few green leaves were tossing back and forth on the air like scraps of paper. He wasn't going to trap her, that was all there was to it. He closed his eyes and tried to imagine himself as a wise old man, looking at this boy from a great distance, and wondering what advice he could possibly give.

Then he stood up, pulled his trowel from his belt, and started digging. When the hole was ready, he set the trap and carefully lowered it in. But he pulled the little round pan—where the cat's foot would step to trip it off—up as high as it would go. He scooped up the loose sandy dirt and sifted it between his palms down onto the trap. The stream of dust slowly filled up the space under the pan, then all around it, and Jesse nudged in little bits of damp mud and packed them there. To make that trap go off, Paw would have to hit it with a rock! Pleased with his work, Jesse finished the job, disguising the trap to make it look like just another stretch of the trail. This was the part he enjoyed.

As a finishing touch, Jesse stood up and urinated in the grass on both sides of the set. There! He said softly. If *that* doesn't warn her, nothing will.

He placed the two sticks just before the pan—for her to step over, and for Paw to spot—then he brushed his own tracks away and left. He set two more traps the same way on nearby trails and started walking slowly back toward camp.

The storm threatened and rumbled, bruised-bottom clouds scooting low over the windy trees. A few big warm raindrops hit Jesse on the neck. As he came near camp, he decided to sit down on a fallen cypress log and wait for the storm to strike. The air felt good, cleansing, and he was proud of his tricks with the steel traps.

Except for the occasional raindrops, there was just the wind and darkness of the storm. A few cracks of lightning spidered across the sky, but the sheets of pouring rain didn't come. Jesse sat on the cypress, enjoying the wind, until it began to get dark.

When he came into camp, Aunt May was working around the open stove, getting supper ready for them all, and Paw waved from his trailer steps. He still held a bottle.

Bean was back from his whiskey run and stood beside Paw giving his report. Robert Elmer caught Jesse's eye and motioned to follow him. They eased to the far end of the clearing, away from Paw, and stood in the evening shadows of the trees.

"Jesse?" Robert Elmer said. He was tall and had an Indian face, hard cheekbones and dark skin and hair. He didn't look like the rest of them.

"Yeah? What is it?"

"You've heard me mention Gloria?"

"A time or two."

"My girl."

"So?" Robert Elmer always made Jesse nervous because he never seemed to talk to Jesse unless it was to tease him.

"Well, you know Aunt May got us a job offer, all of us. Down at Evans' sawmill."

"I know."

"Well, I *got* to go down there. Gloria's too hard to keep an eye on from up here. You get me?"

"I guess."

"Well, Paw won't want us to go, but I *got* to. And I want you to help with him."

"How? He doesn't listen to me."

"Wouldn't you like to go?"

"Sure."

"You could do the work. I'd show you."

"I'm not worried about that."

"Here's all you got to do," Robert Elmer said softly. "Tell Paw you'd like to try it, and you'll give him your pay. Then I'll say I have to go along to keep a good watch on you."

"Robert Elmer!" Jesse said. "I won't do that!"

"I'd make it worth your while."

"How?"

"Fix you up with Gloria's girl friends. How'd you like some of that?"

"No thanks, brother."

"Never did anything like that, did you?"

"Supper!" Aunt May called.

"We better go, Robert Elmer."

"Listen!" He caught Jesse's arm and his grip was tight. "You do what I ask."

Jesse waited for him to let go.

"Do what I ask or you'll be sorry. I mean it."

"Supper!" she cried. "Hurry up!"

Robert Elmer released Jesse and strutted toward the food.

Jesse stood there, disgusted. He wanted that job in town so bad he could taste it.

He was too angry to eat. He remembered the times when they had enjoyed meals as a family. But he turned and walked the other way.

He eased along a deer trail, twisting to avoid the briars. A hundred yards away, he sat on the cypress tree again. He pulled his feet up in case the snakes were moving.

Far off in the swamp, he heard the mellow cackle of a great horned owl.

He smiled and imitated it. He just called softly, who-hoo-who-hoo, and waited.

There was a sharp answer a quarter mile away.

Then another.

The first owl flew in near him: he heard its wings

in a tall leafless snag that was outlined dimly against the sky. Just a single degree of brightness was all that was left of the sunset. He faced east, the darkest direction, and called, who-*who*-oo, a little more ambitiously.

The owl above him was quiet, but just out in the swamp another one called. He answered, briefly, on top of its last note. That did the trick. Owls came flying in and cackling from half a mile away. Their hollow loudspeaker voices rang down the wet, early spring woods, the trees still bare enough to reflect the sharp sounds like walls.

Jesse smiled. The owls were cold, not creatures you could pet, but he loved their excitement and the different rich sounds they could make. Their challenging, overlapping voices, so raw and smooth at the same time, were a kind of music to him.

Then far away in the swamp, a scream began.

Quickly climbing, louder and higher, harsh in the middle now, like the scream of a woman, then it began falling off, clear and musical as it disappeared and still lingered in his ears.

A bobcat.

It filled up the dark silence and he sat perfectly still, listening to his heartbeat. He needed to think about his mother's bobcat. It was such a strange new idea to him, and he felt that it held some kind of secret, some important news, if he could just turn it over and look at it the right way.

Chapter 4

The next morning Aunt May gave them a breakfast of scrambled eggs with wild onion and garlic chives. As she was cleaning up they saw a man walking out of the woods, on the overgrown logging road.

It was the sheriff, Potts Riggins. He was tall, with a pouchy face and belly, and big tatooed arms. He wore khaki work pants and short-sleeved shirt, and except for his badge and pistol he looked like a mill worker.

"Riggins!" Paw cried with a smile. "You forgot what I told you!"

The sheriff stopped twenty yards from them and looked uncertain of his next move.

"I ain't forgot nothin, Twaint. I come to tell you somethin you need to know."

"Yes," Paw said loudly and pleasantly, "you slipped up and forgot."

Riggins wiped his mouth nervously.

"Now listen, Watersmith," he said irritably, "ain't no man got the right to say the law can't walk up on him."

"But I said it, didn't I?"

"Yes, I reckon you said it. But you ain't got a phone. How we supposed to get hold of you?"

"I guess you ain't!" Paw laughed and laughed, and Jesse waited to see what was next.

"Never mind that," Riggins said, "I got somethin to tell you."

Twaint's smile faded. He stared at the sheriff and waited.

"They're gearing up in town for another election."

"You in trouble?"

"Well, I ain't got it made, that's for sure. Preacher's against me, tellin everybody I'm in with the moonshiners."

Paw laughed suddenly in his throat. "Everybody knows that."

"Yeah, Twaint, but I don't have to tell you that even them *drinkin* Baptists will vote against me if I'm too much out in the open."

"Damn hypocrites."

"Now that's so, that's so. But it's a real old system, that you and me ain't gonna change."

Paw looked around and rubbed his palm on his leg.

"Anyway," Riggins said, "folks want a dry county, with moonshine available. Only thing, preacher's got em about half convinced the sheriff who *gives* em that is an outlaw. Twisted as that sounds, you know and I know it's how they are."

"They want their whiskey, I know that."

"Yeah, but I got to ask you to slow it down until after the votin. That ain't long."

"How long?"

"Two months."

Paw spit on the ground.

"If you keep makin runs," Riggins said, "I'm gonna look mighty bad."

"That's your neck."

The sheriff was dark-faced now.

Paw smiled. "You won't have no more job, will you?"

They stared at each other for a long silence in which two jaybirds squawked at each other in a tree.

"Long and the short of it is this, Twaint," Riggins finally said, "if I was to lose this election, you boys would have to talk to a *new* sheriff."

"Yes, indeed."

"*But*, that there new sonofabitch might want more money, or he might rather just put you out of business."

"I'll tell you what," Paw snapped, walking toward Riggins, "I've put me a many a sheriff out of business, is who's put somebody out of business."

The man seemed to wilt under Paw's stare. He looked at the ground.

"Twaint," he said in a tired and patient voice, "all I'm askin for is two months."

"Well, now," Paw said. "*Askin* sounds a lot more like it."

"Sho, Twaint, that's all."

"Well, me and my sons will discuss the matter."

"Go right ahead."

"We'll let you know."

"Ain't necessary," Riggins said, regaining his composure a little, "if I see Robert Elmer and Bean makin them deliveries, or if I don't, either way I'll know."

"Very well then," Paw said, sounding pleased with himself.

"Good day," Riggins said.

"Sho."

When the deputy was gone everybody was busy, avoiding Paw. Bean chopped stovewood for Aunt May without being asked. He set the dry sections of oak on end, swung the axe high and tilted it expertly at the last second, making a fine pistol shot sound and sending the pairs of logs spinning.

Robert Elmer took the five-gallon canvas bag and went off to the spring. And Jesse got a hammer and set about resetting tent stakes loosened by the previous evening's wind.

But Paw himself seemed strangely good-humored. He got out his sharpening stone and his skinning knife, and squatted on the balls of his feet near the woodpile. He smiled as he studied his blade, pulling it carefully first one side then the other, stopping every few strokes to moisten the stone with a few drops of oil from a bent can.

"Boys," Paw finally said.

Bean stood still and Jesse walked over to the woodpile.

"You heard it just like I did."

"Yes, sir," Bean said.

"It ain't good news, but we ain't gonna let it get us down."

He kept scraping the knife.

"I been gettin a good price on venison. Best cuts goin to the cafes, and the rest goin for dog food. Dog food prices are flyin, so what the hell," Paw said. "Really. I mean, they can stop us from one thing, but they can't stop us from another, can they?"

"No, Paw," Jesse said. He was grateful Paw wasn't drinking.

"We'll just kill a few more deer, right Bean?"

"Uh, yeah Paw."

"And catch a few more skins for the fall. Jesse, you got another week or two."

Paw looked out across the clearing before he went on.

"And it won't be too much longer before there's another fish kill."

"Time for one, ain't it Paw?" Bean said.

"It is. It is." Jesse looked at Aunt May and thought about how much she hated Paw selling rotten fish.

"Listen, Jesse," Bean said, "how about seining to-day?"

"Sure."

"Where you goin?" Paw asked.

"Down in the Mock Orange Slough."

"That thing pretty full?"

"Sho is. And them fish are fightin each other for the air."

"Hell," Paw said, "let's go. Let's *all* go." He got up and went toward his trailer for the seine. Bean grabbed Jesse's arm. "Listen," he said, "we can't sell any more deer, and I'm scared to tell him."

"Why not?" Jesse asked. But Paw was already back, grinning with the net around his shoulders.

They waded in the muddy cool water up to their waists, quiet, tall Robert Elmer holding his corner of the net up and watching the surface nervously, Bean following on the bank with the long-handled dip net to separate quickly any snakes from the mass of trapped fish. Jesse and Paw waded with the other corner of the seine.

On their first pass they got a bucketful of bluegills and small catfish. They wiped the mud and sticks from the net to try again.

"Every time the river floods," Paw said, "it brings us all these here treasures."

"Sho does," Bean said.

"I think it's fine," Paw went on. "I think it's right nice of the old river."

A big fish swirled on the brown surface and they raised the seine quickly. It was a five pound bass and they were all grinning as they lifted him onto the weedy bank and watched him jump and flop and wave his gills.

"Aunt May'll like that!" Jesse said.

"What a fish!" Bean added.

"We not doin bad," Paw said. "No we not."

They all smiled in silence as they secured the bass with a bootlace through his lower lip and tied him down in the bucket with the smaller fish. If he was loose he might jump out and roll down the slope into the water again. It had happened to them once and they never forgot Paw's rage.

"Let's hit it!" Paw said.

They straightened out the seine and waded slowly into deeper water.

This time when they eased the corners up they felt a great weight in the center, and at first they thought they had a floating log. Then it was moving toward Robert Elmer and he was backing away and Paw yelled, "Don't you let go! Whatever you do, don't let go this sonofabitch!"

Robert Elmer's face was hard angles already but the bones stuck out through dark skin and he got his tight straight mouth like he always wore into fights. Just the mouth of the creature was showing and the jaws slammed chop-chop so loud that Robert Elmer's knuckles turned white. The rough back of the thing showed now and they all thought it was an alligator.

"I need to let go, Paw," Robert Elmer said. He never begged, and it was a strange voice in which he managed to ask.

"Not yet, boy! Not yet!"

He was backing toward the bank but the ragged back and the chopping big jaws were coming at him faster than he was walking.

"We got to see this thing!" Paw said, grinning.

"No, Paw! Now this is enough! Say I can let go!"

"You chicken, son?"

The question seemed to stop the creature itself, and they all waited motionlessly for an instant, Jesse trying to figure whether Paw was kidding or really testing Robert Elmer. Then it was swimming again and Robert Elmer yelled, "Paw!" but he never took his eyes from the moving water.

"Let go Robert Elmer!" Jesse yelled. "Let go! Let go!"

Robert Elmer looked at Paw once and saw his father unsmiling and daring him to do it.

Then the monster surfaced two feet from Robert Elmer's tight trembling hand and they all saw it was a huge alligator snapping turtle. It was over three feet long and its head was as big as a child's, floating square and malevolent on the surface. Its shell was covered with ragged ridges.

"Lift!" Paw cried, and they heaved their arms high, turning the turtle, and they hurried through the bottom mud to the near bank, and hauled the creature tangled and upside down and hissing and chopping into the weeds.

"I don't believe that!" Bean cried.

"Biggest one I ever seen," Paw said.

He held his own upside down palm near the turtle's foot and they were the same size, with the claws an inch long and the thing opening and closing like the hand of a witch.

Robert Elmer stood towering over the turtle, dripping and muddy up to his chest, not saying a word.

Paw was looking at him and laughing quietly, then louder.

"You sho held your ground, boy! I never seen the like of that! Didn't he?" He turned to Bean and Jesse. "Didn't he hold his ground?"

"He flat did," Bean said, chuckling.

Even Jesse began to smile.

"But *you*," Paw said to Jesse angrily, "you hollered at him to quit! I heard you, too! Told him to disobey his Paw."

"Aw, Paw," Bean said.

"No, no! A time like this, we find out what everybody's made out of. Them damn people in town, most of them never find out. But once in a while, when you don't expect it, you get a look."

Robert Elmer broke the tension.

"What you want to do with him, Paw?"

They all looked at the great snapper, writhing in the net on his back.

"We could sell him to the fish store, couldn't we?" Robert Elmer said. "Make a lot of steaks."

"We'd have to be mighty careful," Paw said. "You boys may not get out of these woods enough to know about it, but them things are now *highly* protected by the law."

"Really?" Bean asked. "I was thinking Aunt May could flat cook us some stews from that sucker."

"She could, couldn't she?" Paw said.

"Let's let him go," Jesse said. "We'll get some little ones for the pot."

"Let him go?" Robert Elmer said. "Let him go and us have to wade in there again?"

"He could take off your foot, couldn't he?" Bean laughed.

"More than that," Paw said.

The turtle kept struggling, waving his head in circles in a slower and slower rythm.

"Aw," Paw said, "we might let him go."

"No, Paw!" Robert Elmer said. "I say no!"

"Look out now, son. You doin good so far today. Don't push it."

"I want to eat him," Bean said.

"I'll tell you what I'd like to do," Paw said. "I wish we could get him to town just to show them folks. If some of them saw him, they'd come closer to stayin out of our swamp, wouldn't they?"

"They sure would," Bean said. "But how could we get him there? He must weigh two hundred pounds."

"I bet he does," Paw said. "He's the dadgumdest thing I ever saw. I think I want to let him go."

"Paw!"

"Hush, Robert Elmer. You don't have to kill every damn thing in the woods."

"But—"

"Hush! Sit down and rest a minute, let's think it over."

Jesse waited, hoping and afraid to say any more.

"Paw," Bean said, "I got some bad news to tell you, and I reckon I'll get it over with."

"Oh?"

"Yes, sir. I hate to tell this."

"Spit it out."

"Well, when I took the whiskey to the fish store yesterday, that feller said to tell you some people in Birmingham got caught servin deermeat in a cafe."

"And?"

"And, to save himself from going to jail, he told em it was *us* that sold it to him. Riggins ain't heard about it yet, but he will soon."

They were all silent, and the only sound was the turtle, moving its head in slow circles in the mud.

Jesse stared at the giant alligator snapper. He understood Bean's wanting to eat it, and Robert Elmer's wanting to sell it. That was all they knew about animals, all Paw had taught them. Aunt May had told Jesse about the massive rare turtles, how they live deep in a few rivers, and almost never appear in hill swamps. They live a long long time, she had said, and it's only right to let them go on living. There are plenty of common turtles around for soup.

They waited until Paw said, "And?"

"And that will shut the deermeat business down tight. Won't be a dollar in it before November."

Paw looked out over the slough a long time.

Jesse saw the cords in the back of his neck swell up and flex in and out.

"So we can't sell whiskey," he finally said, "and we can't sell deermeat."

Nobody answered him.

"What are we supposed to do now?" he said angrily.

The birds whistled softly to each other high above, where sunlight played on the tops of the tall thick trees.

Paw suddenly stared at the moving turtle, focusing on it as tensely as a cat on a mole.

He came to his feet and walked quickly to it, drawing his skinning knife from its sheath, and before Jesse realized what he was going to do he cut off he creature's head.

They had been gone for an hour.

Paw had carried off the bucket of fish and the torn seine to camp.

Robert Elmer and Bean had followed him with each side of the heavy turtle, dark blood marking the way behind them.

Jesse sat without tears beside the head which still moved its jaws slowly now and then, as if trying to taste something for the last time. So Aunt May would be cooking him after all.

He wondered how long it took to make the old turtle. And he wondered simply what difference it made after all when a thing died. It happened so matter-of-factly, like falling leaves or even more like the casual moving of a branch in the wind.

He wondered how life could be so tense and full of struggles and death be so natural as to seem almost innocent.

Still he couldn't convince himself of any natural order or sense to it, and he was left after the wide circle of his thoughts with a blind anger toward Paw that was greater than anything he'd felt before.

Bean had warned him long ago, that the only way to get their father's respect was to fight him, or at least offer to . . .

"But you can't fake it," Bean said. "When you threaten Paw you got to mean it."

"Is that what you did?"

"Me, and before me Robert Elmer. When we got big enough, and fed up enough."

"You actually fought him?"

"Robert Elmer traded a few licks. You know how big he

is. But the thing is this, and remember it: I didn't care anymore whether I was big enough or not. It didn't even matter to me if I killed him or he killed me. Do you understand?"

"I don't think so."

"You got to reach that point. You got to not care. If you care, he'll know it and he'll whip you or scare you to death."

"How can you not care?" Jesse asked.

"You have to answer that for yourself. I didn't understand it until he slapped me the last time and I just had to stand up."

"Does he know all this?"

"You mean is he just testing us?"

"Yeah."

"I don't know. Hell, don't ask me . . ."

Jesse had figured he was a coward, and Bean was not. But how could he face Paw yet, until he got bigger?

He dug a deep hole in the mud with his knife and buried the alligator snapper's head.

The body might be carried away to be food for Watersmith mammals, but the spirit of the old turtle, if there was a spirit, would remain here by the muddy slough.

There was something in the snapper's death that helped Jesse, gave him strength, and he reached inside himself to find it, drag it out into the sunlight. He felt guilty at first for the feeling, but he pulled at the thing and when he saw it he smiled a hard smile: his father was that cold, that sudden; it cut a great distance between him and Jesse.

As long as Jesse cared, Paw's coldness and meanness mattered too much. Jesse wanted, so much, to be close to his father, kept trying again and again.

But Jesse felt older and tougher today.

He looked at the grave of the turtle's soul and felt the tight lines of his own face, not the frightened boy worried sick over his secret bobcat, but more the face of his own brothers and even of Twaint.

He got to his feet and set off in the swamp, unafraid of snakes and squinting his eyes in newfound recklessness and bitterness. He felt like a Watersmith for the first time.

Chapter 5

Jesse walked into camp angrily. Only Aunt May was in sight, laying a fire in the open cookstove.

"Where is he?" Jesse said. "Didn't they come in here?"

Then he saw the huge turtle shell, upside down, and a line of fresh steaks lying inside it.

"Calm down, honey," Aunt May said. "Bean and Robert Elmer went down to the fish store with the rest of the meat. And your paw just took off."

"Where? I've got something to tell him."

"Wait, son. Not like this." She tried to touch his forehead to calm him but he jerked away. "Jesse," she said softly, "he grabbed up his rifle and took it with him. You don't want to mess with him now."

"No," Jesse said, trembling, "he's the one who doesn't want to mess with me."

"Well," she said, "*I* don't know where he went. At least help me with this fire before you run out of here. In fact, if you will, lay me another one over by the oak tree. I've got so much meat I need to smoke some before it goes bad."

Jesse stood there breathing hard and trying to think clearly. He knew Aunt May was chattering on in hopes he would settle down and forget hunting Paw. "I'll help you, Aunt May," he said, "if you need me. I don't have to tell him now. I'm not going to change, though. I'll tell him the same thing tonight."

"What on earth, honey?" she asked, touching his arm gently. This time he didn't pull away.

"I'm leaving here. I've made up my mind. No matter what he says or does. I want you to go, too."

She closed her hands thoughtfully, and looked at him a moment. "I see."

"Yes, ma'am. I'm going to take that job you got me. And if he tries to tell me—"

"Yes?"

"I don't know!" he said, embarrassed. "I don't know what I'll do. But I don't care what happens to me anymore. If you'll just come, too, so he can't take it out on you . . . Will you?"

"Let's take a little walk, Jesse. Let me think on this." She took a big can of black pepper and shook it heavily over the turtle steaks to keep flies away. Then she held Jesse's hand and led him slowly out of the camp.

They passed through cool, sharp-leaved cane, down into the shadows along a sandy creek.

"Jesse," she said, "when he came in a while ago, he got a whiskey jar and sat down on the steps of his trailer."

"That's nothing new."

"No, but Bean came over and told me about the

turtle, how you wanted to save it." Jesse looked
away. "Now, son, I knew I was takin a chance, but
Bean had told me what he said—about the end of the
deermeat business—"

"Yes, ma'am?"

"Well, I walked right up to Twaint and I told him
about the jobs in the mill."

"And what did he say?"

"He just looked at me. For a long time. I got to
wonderin whether he heard me at all."

"Then what happened?"

He picked up the fruit jar and drank that whiskey
like it was spring water. Then he threw it down,
went inside the trailer, came out with his rifle."

Aunt May stopped talking and looked at Jesse. "He
walked right past me into the woods. I have no idea
what he's up to."

"It doesn't matter to me," Jesse said sadly, "my
mind is set. Only thing I want to hear is that you're
coming too."

"If I do, son, it'll upset him that much more."

"But—"

"No, listen. I could stay a little while, and just see
how he takes it. If he ain't too bad, I'll ease on down
in a few days. But if it goes the other way, I'll try to
hold him back here."

"I'd worry about you all the time."

"Yes, but don't you see? As soon as he gets *used* to
it, I can come too."

Jesse looked at her as if she was hiding something.
"Do you promise?" he asked.

"*Certainly*. You go on to town, now, I think it's a good idea. You're to stay at Miss Elmilly's, not out with your brothers. Allow me a little time, let's say two weeks, and I'll come walking up to Elmilly's with my bag over my shoulder."

They both smiled and she patted his arm. "Another good thing about this," she said, "is getting you away from those brothers of yours."

"You think so?"

"Ain't it plain? The way Robert Elmer lives, I don't think he'll make it to be as old as Twaint."

"You don't?"

"No, I sure don't. Twaint has some way about him that makes people put up with him, you know that. But Robert Elmer is just a mean dog and he makes enemies that ain't afraid of him."

"Sometimes Bean is real nice to me, then Robert Elmer comes around and Bean acts just like him."

"Bean never could make up his mind about anything. When he was little, if Tanya wanted to keep him in the yard she'd give him two or three things to play with. He never could settle on which one he wanted, so he'd stay close to them all."

Jesse laughed.

They stopped and listened to a hawk, upset over something, off in the swamp.

"This reminds me of walking with your mama, when she was about your age. We used to talk about all our hopes and wishes. Fine thing we all came to, though."

Jesse listened closely.

"We all figured she would get away, make something of herself. I guess she was the hope we all had after we started giving our own hopes away. You get to a point, Jesse, where all of a sudden you think you're not so special."

"You do?"

"Well, *you* haven't gotten there yet, young man."

A woodpecker landed in the hackberry above them and hammered joyfully with such racket that Aunt May waited. Finally it gave its screeching bobble and flew away.

Then they heard a rifle shot. It was close by in the trees, ringing hard and hollow.

They stood straight, close together, listening.

"Twaint," Aunt May said.

"Killing a deer."

"That's it. He's taking it out on a deer."

"Go on back to camp," Jesse said.

"And what are *you* going to do?"

"I'm going to tell him, Aunt May. I'm not afraid anymore."

"No, son! Not with him drinking. Just get your things and head for town. I'll tell—"

"No. You're not covering up for me anymore. I'll do it myself and then I'll come to camp and pack."

"But you're going to worry me to death."

"I can't help that," he said. "Now you go on. This is something I've got to do."

The deer was lying in a patch of pale sand. It was beside a little branch of the creek, where the water ran out of thick cane into the open woods.

Jesse saw its creamy white belly first. He stood behind a sweet gum tree and watched. Finally he made out Paw's figure squatting behind the body.

The man who decides what lives and what dies, Jesse thought.

He felt the same tight lines in his face he had felt after Paw killed the snapper.

He stepped out from behind the tree and walked in long hard steps toward his father.

Twaint watched him coming. He slowly rolled a cigarette from the red can of Prince Albert he carried in his shirt pocket.

Then Jesse was fifty yards from him and Paw had his cigarette going. He was smiling at his son, looking calm and satisfied, still squatting on the balls of his feet and resting his arms across his knees.

The deer lay just in front of him, with the rifle propped against it.

"You heatin up the trail, boy," Twaint said cheerfully.

"Is that right?"

It was all Jesse could think of. Words tangled up inside him as he walked to Paw and stopped.

"Sho. I could see them leaves and canes steamin as you touched em. If you don't cool down, you gonna burn up the woods."

He smiled and his face was round and red and cute.

Jesse looked away.

"Hundred and thirty-seven yards," Paw said quietly and proudly, nodding toward the deer.

"One shot, huh Paw?"

"You bet."

"How far'd he run?"

"Sixty yards."

"Didn't have to finish him off?"

"Naw. He was dead when I got here."

"It is a he?"

"Yeah."

Paw reached over and caught the first joint of the hind leg and lifted it. Jesse saw the snowy white bag of testicles and Paw smiled.

"Too bad we'll never see his antlers," Paw said.

Jesse knotted his fists. "It is too bad, Paw, it sure is."

Paw just shook his head once, smiled slightly, and drew the smoke deeply into his lungs. He was ignoring Jesse's anger.

"Why'd you kill him?"

"Why'd I kill him?" The smile faded. "What's that supposed to mean?"

"You can't sell him. We don't need to eat him."

"Because he belonged to Will Evans. That enough reason for you?"

"I reckon not, Paw. Not for me."

"Listen at Jesse! Latest thing I hear, boy, Evans wants us all to come work for him. *All* of us, you get me? Looks like a few years pass, and Will Evans forgets what happened. I ain't forgot and I never will. And don't you neither."

Jesse stared at the hornless buck. His lines were as graceful in death as ever, frozen against the sand. The shot had taken him just behind the front shoulder, and there was only a little blood. A trickle ran slowly from his nose.

"I am going to town, Paw. I'm going to take that job."

"Do tell." Paw's easy expression faded.

"You can't stop me."

Paw started to speak then held back. His eyes began to twitch. "You'd work for your old man's enemy?"

Jesse opened his mouth but no words came.

"You know how it is with me and him," Paw said.

The hooves of the buck were caked with brown mud in their center split. Jesse kept his eyes there and tried not to listen.

."That man hates me, son."

"If he does, why'd he offer us a job?"

"Wants to trick me into somethin. I don't know what."

"I'm going, Paw. You can't stop me."

"Know what you remind me of?" Paw said in a thin voice.

"What?"

"Your mother. When she started to double-cross me."

"What are you talking about, Paw?"

"Tanya was an ungrateful woman, Jesse, just like you. No 'preciation for all I done. Tried to raise you right, taught you—"

"Shut up, Paw!" It made him feel crazy to hear that. "You've got no right, Paw," he said. "No right."

Jesse turned and walked away. But Paw said, "Son?" He said it softly and Jesse stopped. "Come back here a minute, would you please?"

Jesse turned and Paw was standing up, holding his rifle loosely in his arms. He was smiling.

Jesse's face and ears turned hot.

"Would you step back for a second, boy?"

Jesse lifted one foot and set it forward, then another.

"This here sawmill job you want so bad . . ." Paw smiled.

"Yeah?"

"You know, a bad man's money spends the same as a good man's money."

"What?"

"Go on and take that job, son!" he said brightly. "I was gonna give you permission myself. Change might do us all good."

Jesse stood there, studying Paw's harmless looking face.

"Yes, sir!" Paw said. "Just what we need, a little cash money to tide us over the election. Remember what I said about Evans, boy, and don't never trust him. The way I understand it, he wants you boys in the mill, and me on his timber cutting crew. Now that means I might not see you every day. But don't worry." Paw grinned and his blue eyes danced. "I'll be checking on you. You won't never be far away from your Paw."

PART II

In the Town

Chapter 6

The three brothers walked through the swamp at sunup, Bean and Robert Elmer carrying their big folded tents over their shoulders, with their clothes in ragged brown suitcases bouncing in their hands. Jesse had his things in an old green army bag Aunt May had given him, but he left his tent behind.

Before seven o'clock they made the four miles to Will Evans' sawmill. It was set up in the enormous field on the woods' edge. A man wearing khakis and a stained straw hat pulled low over his eyes watched them come.

"The Watersmiths, I believe?" he said. He was medium-height, well built and had a face used to looking at others seriously.

"Yes, sir," Bean said. "We ready to git it!"

"Fine. You may stow your gear over there." He pointed to a lone, lush catalpa tree standing apart from the mill. "Later on we'll show you where to set up."

"Yes, sir."

"Now, you are?"

"Bean. The one and only."

"And this would be?" He looked at Robert Elmer.

"Robert Elmer Watersmith. Paw said he'll be down in a few days."

"I see. And?"

"That's Jesse," Bean said. "He's the little brother of this crew."

"Where is your tent, young man?" Mr. Evans said.

"I'll be staying in town."

"All right." He turned to his mill, suddenly distracted. "We start at eight. You two—" he indicated the older brothers—"take up places at the end of that chain. The boys will show you what to do. Jesse, come over here."

He led the way to a huge pile of weathered stacking sticks, used to separate boards so they would dry and not rot. They were eight feet long and one inch square, jumbled and tangled, sticking out in all directions.

"Do you have work gloves?"

"No, sir."

"I see."

He pulled a pair of cloth and canvas gloves from his hip pocket and handed them over.

"Get some of your own today."

"Yes, sir."

"Put all the sticks in that rack. There are two more piles behind the mill. After that, come see me."

"Yes, sir."

"Jesse?"

"Sir?"

"How old are you?"

"Sixteen."

"Do you know how to work?"

"Yes, sir." He smiled.

"We'll see."

Mr. Evans seemed about to say something more, then changed his mind and walked away.

The morning sun was full and bright, burning off the cool dewy smell on the grass and green lumber, and reflecting like wet fire on the tin roofs over the mill machinery.

Jesse started quickly to his job. Mr. Evans was such a . . . he couldn't think of the word . . . such an *orderly* man. He knew exactly what he was doing.

Jesse pulled out the first long stacking stick. He tossed it into the rack.

He had already finished the pile when he heard the sawmill start. As he walked around behind the mill to the other piles he heard the logs flipping on the carriage, landing with huge thuds, and the fierce treble whine of the sawblade as it began slicing boards from the logs.

The smell of fresh sawdust was fine.

Jesse worked his way quickly through the next pile, and was drenched in sweat. He looked over his shoulder once, wiping his brow, and saw Mr. Evans watching him. Then he tore into the next tangle of sticks as hard as he could, and was almost out of breath as he finished it.

He looked up, and saw that a long, flat-bed trailer-truck had pulled into the yard, and some men were tearing down the stacked lumber next to it and banding the tight packages of boards with long ribbons of thin steel. They must have been caught off guard, not expecting the truck so early, because they were rushing to get the lumber ready for loading. Each time they finished tearing down a bunk, or package of lumber, they left a new pile of the jumbled stacking sticks.

Mr. Evans motioned Jesse over and pointed to the new piles. "Watch out for the fork truck," he yelled.

The mill was steadily rolling, the carriage traveling back and forth, the sawyer flipping his logs in place as the bark slabs were cut off the sides, then sending them again to meet the high-speed whirling sawblade. The hours slipped by.

Jesse felt the hot late-morning sun on his face and neck. The dirt was powder dry around the mill, and a fine cloud of red dust mingled with sawdust had caught in the sweat on his skin. He rushed through pile after pile of the sticks, and he began to feel the dust in his mouth and down his throat when he heard a voice close behind him.

"Ho now, young man."

He turned quickly around, breathing hard and squinting into the blazing sun.

"You got to learn to *work*," the old black man said.

"What do you mean?" Jesse said, a little resentfully, and afraid he was not going fast enough.

"Wellsuh, the way you stackin them sticks, you be ready to fall down befo lunchtime."

Jesse stared blankly at him.

"I seen em drop," he said, "many a time."

The black man stooped and picked up a stacking stick, took a couple of steps, and deftly tossed it onto the rack.

"You want to last," the man said. "What's yo name?"

"Jesse."

"Jus *Jesse?* Thas all?"

"Watersmith. Those are my brothers over there."

Jesse was a little nervous that he had stopped work. He glanced around.

"Old man Twaint Watersmith's boy?" The black man, who was small, heavily muscled, and stooped over, made a surprised face.

"That's right," Jesse said, starting back to work. He hated to be identified. His name was like a weight.

"I know him all right," the man said. "Ain't a soul *don't* know yo daddy."

Jesse went on working, not looking at the man. He tried to slow down a little, feeling embarrassed at being corrected.

"He a *rough* one," the man went on, moving to help Jesse. "Tell me he *stay* back in them swamps."

"That's right."

"My name is Nathan Brown. I been with Mr. Evans for twenty years, ever since he started up to sawmillin in this country."

Jesse thought, well, at least maybe he won't get me fired with all this talk. The black man was so solemn in everything he did, that Jesse didn't know whether to take his advice as a criticism. But he began to relax.

"You still goin too fast," Nathan said. "You gonna find out, bout three this afternoon."

"All right."

Jesse had never been around black people much, and he had heard them cursed all his life. He expected them to be terrible, though he wasn't sure just how. But Nathan was helping him, and seemed gentle.

"Mr. Evans a good man," he was saying. "He treat you right if you work. Don't matter to him what yo name is."

Jesse flushed.

"You jus start today?"

"Yeah. Me and my brothers. Bean and—"

"I reckon I know yo brothers, all right."

Jesse worked on, wondering what he meant.

"They some of them, what I call, *white* cowboys."

"I guess they'd like to be."

"Thas it. Thas it. You look to be a little dif'ent."

"I reckon."

"Yo brother Robert Elmo, he got in a terrible fight with a feller named Perkins, works here. Bout two, three weeks ago."

"I heard."

"He cut that feller. He been in the hospital over in Tuscaloosa ever since."

"I didn't know that."

"Fightin over some gal down at The Water Hole.

Some gal that don't care bout either one of them."

"Water Hole?"

"Thas a joint. It's a concrete block building with naked women painted all over it."

"Oh."

"Ain't no fit place to be goin. Some the colored boys was up in the air cause it was only for white folks. But I told em it sho don't make me proud to see em bustin to get in a joint like that."

Jesse thought about this as they worked in silence, side by side, for a long time. Then the sawmill engine cut off and the belts whipped to a slow stop. Nathan dropped his stick and stood up.

"Lunch time. You bring any food?"

"No."

It was the first time Jesse had thought of it. Now, suddenly, he felt weak and hungry.

"Got any money?"

"No. I just came out of the swamp."

"Well, if you start right now"—he pointed toward town—"you can go to the store and git back in time."

Nathan reached into his pocket and pulled out a dollar. It was damp and wrinkled.

"You kin give it back payday."

"That's all right," Jesse said, hesitantly.

"*Go on*, white boy!" Nathan said irritably. "You got to eat." He put the bill in Jesse's hand and turned toward the mill.

"Thanks."

Nathan just waved his hand slightly, without looking back.

That afternoon the sun seemed to grow hotter and hotter. The dust was caked on Jesse's neck and down in his shirt. He kept pulling the stacking sticks and squinting his eyes. They stung with sweat, dust, and the glare of the sun. The men stayed just ahead of him all afternoon, taking down lumber stacks and leaving piles of stacking sticks behind. Mr. Evans walked briskly past a few times. He was busy and didn't say anything.

When the mill finally shut down at five o'clock, Jesse sat heavily on his half finished rack of sticks. He needed to rest.

Bean came over to him.

"What you say, hoss?"

"You're in a good mood, I see."

"Why not? Maybe you ain't thought of it, little brother, but from now on, every night is Saturday night!"

He laughed and slapped his leg. Jesse didn't smile. He was sore and tired. As far as he was concerned, Saturday was no different from any other night.

"Me and Robert Elmer goin down to the swimmin hole at the creek. Wanta come?"

"That sounds good to me," he said.

They walked about a mile to the wide place in the creek that was the town swimming hole. Three little boys were sitting on the bank, and when they saw the Watersmiths they screamed and took off. Bean and Robert Elmer laughed so hard they nearly fell down.

"I reckon that's the same ones was here the last time." Bean said.

"Musta been," Robert Elmer said.

"What did you do to them?" Jesse asked.

"Aw, not much," Bean said. "We just asked em real polite if we could have the place to ourselves."

"One of em was a smart mouth little devil," Robert Elmer said.

Bean laughed. "So we dunked him a few times."

"What was that we told him?" Robert Elmer asked.

"Oh yeah, we told the little sucker it was Halloween, and we was just dunkin him in the apple barrel!" They both laughed as they pulled off all their clothes and dived in.

Jesse stripped and followed them. The cold water down deep felt wonderful.

After he swam up and down the water hole, and washed the dust from his hair, he stood waist high and looked up at the sky.

He found himself near Robert Elmer, with Bean swimming far up the creek.

Robert Elmer's hard-boned Indian face was stark against the blue sky, and his black hair was slicked back with the water.

"Robert Elmer," Jesse said. "I got to ask you something."

"Sho, boy, go right on."

"Well, do you know how our mother drowned?"

Robert Elmer looked surprised and smiled.

"Nobody knows that," he said. "I tried to find out, and so did Bean. Everybody's got a different story."

"Like what?"

"Oh, Lord. Let's see. Aunt May used to say she died. That's what she always told me when I was a kid."

"Died from what?"

"First it was just died, in her hammock. Later on it was drowned in Bluebottom Creek."

"And what about Paw? What did he say?"

"He used to claim she ran off. Aunt May says it ain't true."

"But he changed his story?"

"Well, once when he was drunk as a skunk he said she prob'ly did drown, because the creek sho was flooded bad enough."

"He said that?"

"Yeah. No telling what really happened. But I always figured he was there when she went in. And you can figure the rest of it for yourself."

"You mean he pushed her?"

"Won't a soul on this earth ever know that, Jesse."

Bean emerged suddenly from the water, right beside them. He grinned.

"Little brother," Bean said, "we seen you talkin to that black."

"What was the sonofabitch tellin you?" Robert Elmer said.

"Aw," Jesse said, "he told me I was workin too fast. That I'd—"

"Lord God, yes," Robert Elmer said, looking away with his level hating stare, as if he were planning some personal revenge.

"No!" Jesse said. "You don't understand. He was just—"

"You the one don't understand," Bean said. "They will try their *dadgumdest* to get you to slow down. They'll tell you it's bad for you to work. What the hell? If they get fired they just git on the welfare."

"You see em all day long," Robert Elmer said, "sittin on the porch. Sittin there on the porch, that's all. If he tries to talk to you, Jesse, tell him to go to hell."

"Aw, he was all right."

"That's a bad sign, ain't it Robert Elmer?" Bean said.

"Sho."

"Now brother, you don't know them like we do. We have worked with em, fought with em—you ain't never safe around one. Would you say that's true, Robert E.?"

"Wish it warn't."

"We'll steer you right," Bean said to Jesse. "You just stick with us."

"Okay. Look, I got to go. I'm staying at Miss Elmilly Robertson's."

"I know that old lady well," Robert Elmer said.

"I know her, too," Jesse said.

"She used to be a schoolteacher. She's about half a preacher." Bean laughed. "Give him a week and he'll be out in the field with us!"

By the time Jesse walked back to the mill and got his bag of clothes, then walked to town, he was worn out and sweaty again. The familiar old town—dreary buildings built in the thirties and forties, sagging against each other in their faded, flaking coats of pink and tan and light green paint—was still and quiet. Jesse figured the stores had closed up when the saw-mill did, and most people were already home for supper. Down the middle of the wide main street was a double lane of parking spaces, their diagonal lines barely visible as ragged spots of worn white paint. There were no cars parked. The telephone and power lines hung low over the street. It was a town that seemed tired to Jesse. He had come there with Aunt May on Saturday shopping trips, and he had good memories of the shade in Miss Elmilly's house—her chocolate milk and brownies—but the rest of it seemed boring. Aunt May told him there were rich folks about—landowners and lawyers and doctors who drove all the way to Columbus or Tuscaloosa to practice—but you don't see them. "They're way back up in the trees," she had said, "tending to their swimming pools."

Miss Elmilly Robertson's house was a small Victorian place with badly peeling white paint and a comfortable wrap-around front porch. The picket fence was almost ready to fall down and it was covered with wild roses in buds about to bloom. Miss Elmilly was sitting on the porch. She was thin as a broomstick and reminded him of a severe, alert hawk, perched high on a telephone pole.

"Hello," he said.

"Hello, yourself, Jesse! It's been a mighty long time."

"Yes, ma'am. Did my aunt—"

"Indeed she did. Just left about an hour ago. And yes, you are welcome to stay here on one condition."

He smiled. "What's that?"

"That you take a bath first thing. You look like a wild Indian."

"Done," he said with a grin. "That sounds good to me."

"Well," she croaked, "hop to it, and when you get out I'll talk to you in the kitchen."

His room was in the back, with a window onto the garden. It was a big, well-loved garden, bounded by a rusty ornamental iron fence. His bathroom was between his room and the kitchen, and as he filled the deep porcelain tub, spidered with elegant cracks here and there, he sniffed the musty old-woman smell of the house and stared at the fixtures. Then he slid down into the warm water and lay still, listening to Miss Elmilly stir around in the kitchen through the wall.

He was glad he wasn't out in the field, sweating, hot, and hungry. Here, knowing he was about to be fed and hoping she could cook like Aunt May, his hunger almost felt good. He closed his eyes for a moment, and thought of the sawmill.

He couldn't believe he could be so relaxed in a new place, but the tiredness and warm water drained his worries away. He was sure his brothers were wrong about Nathan. He heard Nathan's rich voice saying, "I seen em drop, many a time." Over and over again, "I seen em drop . . ." Jesse fell sound asleep in the tub.

Chapter 7

Aunt May slipped down after a few days to tell Jesse what Paw was doing. He had gone to work on Evans' woods crew, guiding the timbercutters into new tracts and running a chain saw. Some nights he stayed in a tent near the job, and others he came back to camp. But he was too tired to bother her, and she wanted to stay in camp a while longer. Jesse tried to argue, but she thought it best. Having Paw out of all their hair *was* about the nicest thing he could think of, so he agreed with Aunt May for the time being.

Jesse would have missed his swamp except for the morning walks to the mill, with the sun well up but still cool, the dewdrops alight in the last minutes before they would evaporate, the huge webs of golden spiders glistening in wetness, and the bright spider's silk itself. He watched each morning come as he worked in the yard, and enjoyed the hot sun which he had learned to tolerate, and the rank sweet smell of the catalpa tree when he sat in the shade at lunch.

Succeeding at the mill and in his new life were

very important to Jesse, and he was afraid his brothers would mess him up if he spent much time with them. For the next few weeks he held himself to a tight routine of work, swimming, when he could avoid them, and coming home to Miss Elmilly's house. The cool damp spring seemed to dry up quickly, and an early hot summer settled down on the town. The lumberyard was blown with fine powdery dust. Jesse worked a little too fast at his stacking-stick job. He wasn't sure about trusting Nathan's advice—maybe the man was allowed to go slower because of his age.

And he worried over what his brothers had said, that "they" were all lazy and would try to get you to be, too.

"What you got today," Nathan asked, looking at his lunch sack, "butterbeans and cheesecake?" He grinned and showed the spaces between his teeth.

"Naw," Jesse laughed. "But it's just as good."

They sat together in the shade of the catalpa tree. The only other shade was in the mill itself, under the open sheds. The rest of the men sat in there, mostly whites, but Jesse didn't like to eat with them. From the beginning his brothers always sat a little apart, and usually made cracks about the other workers. Their talk upset Jesse, and he couldn't swallow his food. He chose to eat alone under the catalpa. But after a week old Nathan came over to him.

"Dogs like to got my fox this mornin," Nathan said.

"Your what?"

"My fox. Prettiest thing you ever seen."

"Is it tame?"

"It? Ain't no *it*. It's a *she*. Little red fox got caught in a trap. Tame as a dog and twice as smart."

"Did you trap her?" Jesse almost said he was a trapper.

"Me? I wouldn't do such a thing to *no* animal. I found her in a trap with her po leg broke. She was lyin down on her side, near bout gone."

"How'd you save her?"

"Wellsuh, now that was a trick. I tangled her in a great big fish net first, and then I wrapped up her jaws with a cord. She scratched the tarnation out of me with them front claws, and I like to gave up. But finally I got her home."

"How'd you get her tame?"

"Same way you tame a human. With food. Took me a whole year, but she finally learnt *who* was bringin her all that good supper every night."

They ate their sandwiches and listened to the sparrows in the tree above them.

"What kind of supper?"

"*Fox* supper. Rabbits. I'd bring my singlebarrel shotgun to the mill, and one way or t'other I'd get me one. My wife like to kill me cause she *love* rabbit. And she *can* cook it. Finally one night I come home with a big one, and we was all hungry. Had my nogood son layin around the house and he ate everything we had. She say, 'Nathan, this the *end*. You jus ain't gonna give that fox no more rabbits. Not with me *and* you hungry.'

"Wellsuh, that's when she got me mad. My old black face musta turned red. That time, now, I had had my little three-footed fox for a year. I near about loved her more than my own *son*, and don't tell me that's a sin because I already *know* it.

"I had to face up, right then, to one of the *pullenest* and *tryinest* moments of my lifetime."

"What did you do?"

"I said to myself, 'Old man, who is this woman to you?' Then I said, 'Who is this here red fox to you?' Now, my wife is a fine woman. I know the difference, too. When I was young I had a wife—" he closed his eyes tightly and snapped his face from side to side— "she run me to the wall. I was out workin two jobs to pay for her high heel shoes, and she was entertainin my friends in the bedroom. I like to jumped in the river more nights than one. *But*, then the Lord seed me through all that, and I married my present wife, Roxanne.

"Well boy, I'm ramblin. But the short of it is, I looked at my wife and then at my little fox, and then Roxanne caught me lookin at the two of em, just like I was decidin which chicken to buy, and when I saw *that* look on her face I chose right quick.

"I rose above the whole thing by offerin to sacrifice my fox. I said, 'Very well. I shall open the door to the cage. If she goes, she goes, and if she cares about this old man, she will stay.' "

Nathan took a big bite on his pickle.

"You opened up the cage door?" Jesse said.

"Unlatched the latch. Stood back. Wife and boy

was watchin. I opened the door. She comes right out, dainty like, walks around the yard and looks it over. Well, we forgot all about that swampbuck rabbit we was fightin over. I had left it lying on the stump. When my foxy comes to it she takes it in her mouth and trots off into the weeds."

"What did your wife do?" Jesse was smiling.

"Roxanne? She didn't have the meanness to run screamin after the po little fox and run her off. She *know* thas what I was lookin for. So she went inside and slammed the door, and I listened to her cryin. But my fox jus ate that supper and come right up to me, and been right by me ever since.

"Po Roxanne. To this very day she ain't sure if I lef that rabbit on the tree stump jus to feed my fox. She quit speakin of the thing a long time ago, but *I* know that she still ain't sure."

"*Did* you?"

Nathan smiled and the sawmill engine kicked in.

"Time to go to work," he said.

Jesse laughed.

As they rose from the shade of the tree, Jesse saw a figure on horseback coming toward the mill from far across the field. He watched as the light gray horse galloped gracefully past the lumber stacks, then the log pile, then the mill itself, a slender girl with long hair on its back. She rode past the mill like a ripple of smoke on a strong breeze.

Nathan caught Jesse's arm and pulled him toward the running sawmill.

"Nathan—"

"Thas Mist Evans girl," Nathan said. "Renly Anne. She some little lady."

When Jesse went back to work for the afternoon he kept thinking about the girl on the gray horse. She seemed separated from the heat and dust of the mill yard, as if that horse were flying along in a pure current of cool air. He thought of how the hawks and turkey vultures drifted in the high wind above the hot swamp.

Mr. Evans came up to him at three o'clock and smiled.

"Jesse," he said, "you stay about one pile behind my loading crew."

Jesse winced into the sun and at the criticism.

"You misunderstand me, son. I mean you go mighty fast."

"Oh. Yes, sir."

"You sure do. Remind me of myself when I was a boy."

Jesse looked at him and smiled.

"Only difference, now," Mr. Evans said, "was *I* had this stacking-stick job when I was six years old."

"You did?"

"Yep. My father put me to work that year, and I've been at it ever since."

"Yes, sir."

"You look a little bit wilty, son," he said.

He pulled a plastic container of capsules from his shirt pocket and gave it to Jesse.

"Salt," he said. "Take one whenever the heat gets to you."

"Thank you, sir."

"I want you to try something new. Come over here."

He led the way to the end of the chain where his brothers had been working since the first day.

"Just stand here and do what Bean does."

There were two chains, one on each side of the lumber, turning slowly and moving the freshly cut boards out of the sawmill. The men on either side pulled them off and separated them by lengths into bunks.

"This is southern yellow poplar," Mr. Evans said, "pretty stuff."

"Yes, sir, it sure is."

"Well, just pull it for a while, get the feel."

Then he was gone.

Jesse settled in to watching the boards come. They were a rich creamy color, almost white in the sap wood, and the dramatic streaks of heart were bright green. He thought it was the most beautiful wood he had ever seen.

"Did you get used to the heat yet?" Bean asked him.

"I reckon."

"Shoot," Robert Elmer said.

"What's eatin you, hoss man?" Bean asked.

"One more hour an a half of this," he said.

He spit brown tobacco juice onto the white board in Jesse's hands.

"Look at his eyes," Bean laughed.

Jesse looked and Robert Elmer's face was darker than usual and haggard.

"The boy burnin it at both ends," Bean said. "He got a clear field with that Perkins woman and he is *flat* takin advantage of it."

Robert Elmer looked at him hard.

"But he forgets to sleep!"

"Bean," Robert Elmer said, "tend to your beans."

"Oh funny!" Bean said, in the same high good mood he seemed to have been in since they left the swamp.

"Jesse," Bean said. "What about *your* female part of life? You ain't doin somethin you shouldn't to that old woman?"

Jesse was disgusted. He didn't answer Bean.

They worked on without talking for a long time.

Jesse pulled the boards and thought how they had seen right through him. How could they know what was on his mind? The girls who lived in town paid him no attention, and he guessed they thought he was too rough for them. They passed Miss Elmilly's in little groups, wearing sandals and jeans and sleeveless blouses with cheap lace ruffles. One or two always wore too much rouge and green eye shadow. He did not know what they were about.

The mill engine came to its slow, belt-flapping stop. Jesse, nearly hypnotized by the steady rhythm of the clean fresh lumber moving slowly on the chains, shook himself.

"I don't think I coulda stood no more," Robert Elmer said, and he flung the sweat from his arms like something despised.

"Oh well," Bean said, "old man's rest is a young man's play! Let's go to town!"

"Bean," Robert Elmer said. He was looking side-ways at Jesse.

"Yeah?"

"I think we need to talk to little brother."

Jesse's stomach turned over lightly in fear.

"Oh yes!" Bean said. "I believe you right."

Jesse looked around and saw that the other mill hands were drifting away, already most of them were a hundred yards off.

"What do you want?" he said to Bean.

"We done tole you the last time," Robert Elmer said seriously, "not to talk to that Nathan."

"We seen him out there under the tree," Bean put in.

"What was he puttin into your head today?" Robert Elmer asked.

"Nothin. He just likes to talk."

"Ain't that just like one of em?" Bean asked, grinning.

"About what, boy?" Robert Elmer stepped toward Jesse. He sounded edgy.

"Aw, he told me about his pet fox. He said it's just like a dog."

Robert Elmer stopped and thought about that one.

"Pet fox," he said softly.

"Just *like* one," Bean said.

"Keeps a fox at home?" Robert Elmer said.

"Yep."

"There's laws against that."

"There are?"

"Yes, there *is*. Sanitation. Rabies. I don't know what all."

"Ain't a one of em ain't outlaws," Bean said.

"You tell him we know all about his fox," Robert Elmer said.

"What does that mean?" Jesse asked.

"You takin his side?"

"*What* side?"

Robert Elmer looked at Jesse so hard that Jesse felt he was invisible and his brother had glared right through him.

"Bean, the boy doesn't even know there *are* sides."

Robert Elmer turned and Bean followed him out of the mill without another word to Jesse.

He sat there and watched them slowly disappear across the big field toward the swimming hole. As he had done so many times before, Jesse tried to ignore them and the knot they left in his stomach. He liked the feeling of the big powerful sawmill machines, so hot and still after their day's grinding. The silence after long hours of the roaring engine, the pounding of logs as they were flipped on the carriage, and the ear-hurting whine of the blade as it bit into fresh wood, slowly descending in pitch as the board was severed from the log, and finally trailing off with the last inch of wood—the silence was beautiful. He smelled the worn rubber belts, the floor boards repolished every day with oil and sawdust and men's boots. Jesse walked along the carriage run to the gleaming silver saw, a four foot circle of bright steel.

The last log had been left on the carriage, with its four bark slabs cut off. At this stage it was called a cant, and Jesse stared at it, the creamy white sapwood of poplar looking so clean and fresh in the steamy mill.

Jesse smiled.

The new life was good.

Chapter 8

Two weeks later, after work, Jesse decided to go swimming alone. He crossed the long dry field and was pleased to see the hole empty.

The black clear water shifted brass nails of light across its surface.

He stripped and dove. Three feet down the water turned cool, and he swam as far as he could before shooting up for breath.

The sun blinded him for a moment, and he laughed as a school of fast minnows tickled his legs.

"You havin fun, boy?"

His father's voice came out of the bright sun, out of the sycamore tree spreading from the west bank.

He quickly shaded his eyes and searched for his father.

"Up here, Jesse."

He heard the chuckle in Twaint's throat.

"Didn't I tell you I'd keep an eye out?"

"Yes."

"Well, here I am. I been cuttin down trees until I'm sick of it. How *you* like the job?"

Jesse swallowed, realizing his father wouldn't go away just by his wishing it.

"It's all right."

"Yeah? How about Evans? How's he treat you?"

"Fine."

"You don't say? He don't let you know how he feels, then? Don't you be fooled for a minute. He'll be lookin for a chance to trip you."

"Come down out of the tree, Paw. I can't holler at you like this."

Twaint chuckled in his throat again, and Jesse watched him slowly climb down. He grinned, the late sun on his teeth with the spaces between them, and on his red and tanned round face. His thin gray hair was longer but his beard was freshly shaved. He sat down beneath the tree and curled his long arms around his knees.

Jesse felt foolish naked, but the only way he had to dry off was the air and sun, so he walked near his father and stood in the waist-deep creek.

"Paw," he said slowly and very composed, "I think you're wrong about Mr. Evans."

"I leave you alone and folks take you right in. Listen, boy. In a right world, them what lived in the swamp would own it. I spend my life out there, raisin a family, and I'm just waitin for the day they'll cut every stick of timber down, and tell us to get out."

"Mr. Evans is not a bad man, Paw."

"Evans!" Paw's eyes jumped from side to side. "It's men like him that lay claim to everything. They'd take my huntin away if they could. You know how I feel about that?"

"Yes, Paw, you've told me enough times."

"It makes me feel better than anything I've ever tasted, Jesse, *anything.* Them rich doctors in Tuscaloosa and Columbus, half of them live to hunt deer. They know how I feel. Half the rich folks in this world hunt every chance they get. Don't nobody know why it feels so good. You watch a cat. You feed him all he wants. You think he's gonna quit huntin mice and birds? Hell, no. Huntin is the best thing in this world, son, and I ain't never gonna stop, *never.*"

Jesse looked down at the bright water.

"I see what's happenin behind my back," Paw said. "You better come right to the swamp with me today."

"No! I won't do it!"

"Hold on, don't get so hot. I was just kiddin, son. I see you do like it in town."

Jesse looked down the level creek and watched dragonflies skim the surface.

"I thought you might like to know what your Paw's been up to."

"What?"

"Well, let's see now. We had us a dandy fish kill. I needed you boys after work. I was mighty tired from cuttin trees all day, but May got out there with me and we scooped up nearly three hundred pounds."

Jesse was shocked—Aunt May always hated Paw selling the rotten fish.

"I got the word at the fish store there's a big kill three days upriver, going on right now. If them chemicals come on down here before they dilute, I'm gonna clean up again."

"Paw, I hate that."

"My fish business? Why Jesse, that's what puts food on the table."

"Not much food. I wish you'd do something else."

"Well, you don't like my deermeat trade, you don't care for trapping anymore, let's see . . . you object to the moonshine, don't you?"

"Aw, Paw . . ."

"Yes! I know what that leaves: I can come to town and be a slave for Mr. Evans, like you and your brothers. That what you want for old Paw?"

"I don't want anything bad for you, you know that. I just think . . ."

"What *do* you think? You got so many opinions now you could paper the wall with them."

"I think you must look for these things to do."

"What?" Paw's face was dark red and his voice hard.

"Selling poison fish! How would *you* like to eat in a cafe that served some of them?"

"It's mostly black cafes, don't you know that?"

"Well, so what? You want to poison them?"

"I've known a few could stand it. Matter of fact"— he grinned—"it ain't a bad idea."

"That's sick, Paw."

"What, you love them now?"

"I got me a friend in one, Paw. And ain't nothing wrong with him."

"Who?" Paw snapped.

"Nathan Brown."

"Brown? He's the one got me fired from the mill! Claimed I burnt down his house! I told you that!"

"Well, *did* you burn it down?"

"That snake was hidin a communist in that house. He deserved whatever he got."

"So you did it."

"No, I didn't do it! But I'll tell you one thing: I wouldn't tell you if I did."

"Paw," Jesse said, "how did Mama die?"

"Mama?" He was taken back and he held silent, thinking. His eyes switched like a cat's tail.

"Who's been talkin to you?"

"Why do you have to assume that?"

"Assume? You learnin to talk good, ain't you?"

"What about Mama?" Jesse said angrily.

"She got sick. She was out of her head and she went swimming and drowned."

"Where?"

"In Bluebottom Creek."

Jesse held still. He listened to a bumblebee near his head.

"*Where* in Bluebottom?"

"The old tressel. You know?"

"Yeah, I know."

"Now," Paw said, standing up. He grabbed Jesse's pants and started going through the pockets. "Is there any other damn thing you'd like to know today?"

Jesse started to object, then said only, "No, there's not."

"Good. Because that's all I'm in the mood for. I

send you to town and you lose your manners in a few weeks. No money here, eh?" He tossed the trousers away. "Oh! There is one more thing I bet you'll be interested in."

"What's that?"

"I was talking to the government trapper for this area, ran into him at the river where he was helpin the game warden catch some net men. Anyway, he says they've got a secret potion now that will lure in bobcats to your traps like flies to honey."

Paw stood there grinning, his eyes lit up.

"What do you mean?"

"I don't know what's in it, but just a drop or two will make that old cat hop all over the place huntin it, and he'll trip off the trap quicker than he ever would with our old trail sets."

"You've got this stuff?"

"Not yet, but he's gonna get me a bottle. Won't be long, son! Won't be long!"

Paw waved in a mock gesture of friendliness, laughed hard again and walked off across the field shaking his head to let Jesse know he was still enjoying the joke, even out of hearing.

Jesse dove to the bottom and swam furiously until he thought his lungs would burst.

Then he was walking home in the still early summer dusk.

He was lost in thoughts of his inescapable family when he heard the pickup truck idling beside him.

He looked up quickly into Mr. Evans' calm smiling face.

"Hop in, Jesse," he said.

And he did. The cab smelled of rich pipe tobacco, and a copy of *The Southern Lumberman* lay on the seat.

The truck was new and much wider than any Jesse had ridden in.

"Thanks for the ride," he said. "I went to the swimming hole and I'm tired."

"I bet."

"It sure feels good after work."

"You've been working mighty hard."

"Yes, sir."

"That's fine. There's a generation today that won't work. I've got a friend with a sawmill, he has to confine his cuts to one inch lumber. Two inch lumber is too heavy for his yard crew to lift, according to them."

"My goodness."

"Isn't that something?"

"Yes sir."

"Sawmills are closing down every day because the managers get worn out after a while, trying to find labor."

They pulled onto Miss Elmilly's street.

"They say you grew up in that swamp. Is that right?"

"Yes, sir."

"Interesting. I'd like you to tell me about that sometime."

"You would?" Jesse couldn't believe any man could

be so different from Paw. He watched Mr. Evans'
face; the gray eyes against his tan skin were full of
light.

"Yes. Would you mind?"

"No, sir."

"Good. Tell you what. Why don't you come over
Saturday for lunch? You could meet Ren. Would you
like that?"

"At your house?"

"Of course. Know where it it?"

"No sir, but I'd like to come. I can find it."

"You can, huh?" Mr. Evans smiled as he stopped
the truck. "That's good, then. I'll look forward to it,
Jesse. Sure will."

Chapter 9

Once Jesse turned toward Miss Elmilly's he saw that she had company. There was another old woman in the front porch rocking chair beside her. Then he realized it was Aunt May.

He jumped over the gate and ran up the steps to greet her.

"Shaggy dog!" she cried as she hugged him. "I thought you promised me that you would go to the barber shop!"

"I will," he said. "I just didn't want to spend the money."

"Well, if *that's* the reason," Miss Elmilly put in, "*I* could have loaned it to you."

"You look like a sawmill hand," Aunt May said.

"Yes, ma'am, I am."

"Go and get your bath," Miss Elmilly said. "Your aunt is not going to run off."

"I will. I've got lots to tell you about."

"That's good, son. Hurry back."

Jesse lay in the hot bathwater with a smile on his

face. It was comforting to see Aunt May in town, away from Paw. But he had broken two promises to her. His hair was long and he had not started his lessons with Miss Elmilly.

Every night she had offered, but he had been too tired.

When Jesse put on his clean jeans and shirt, and walked across the living room floor toward the porch, he heard them say his name.

"Jesse ain't *one bit* like the rest of them," Aunt May said. "I don't know if you can see that yet."

Jesse stopped and listened.

"All right, May, you made your point. The question is, what's to become of him now?"

"Well, Elmilly, that's where *you* come into it. I'm countin on you to think of something."

"That will take some thinking," she said. "He's not exactly ready for his own grade in school, you know."

Jesse shifted his weight from one bare foot to the other, and an old pine floorboard cracked.

"Jesse?" Miss Elmilly called.

He stood still.

"He's takin some bath," Aunt May said.

"Hmm? Oh, he always does. He lives in that tub of mine."

"Poor thing."

"I just don't know what to tell you about him."

"He was the smartest child."

"So you keep saying," Miss Elmilly said.

"Well, he *was*. He taught himself to read by the

time he was six. Back in those days we got the paper, and he sat there and read it out loud to me."

Jesse smiled, trying to imagine this.

"The trouble is," Aunt May went on, "there never was much else to read. Oh, he can read better than his brothers, but he's just never read anything. The boy is like a blank page himself. And I'm scared to death what's liable to get printed on it now."

"Well, May, honey, all I can tell you is what I've said before—if he wants to sit down and study, I'll do what I can for him. But I can't *make* him work."

"I know."

They stopped talking then, and Jesse carefully walked backward a few steps, then took loud barefoot strides across the creaky floor toward them. He opened the screen door.

"I can smell him from here." Aunt May said, "but this time it smells like soap, thank heaven."

They all laughed.

"Jesse," Aunt May said, "I want to talk to you."

"I know," he said, "my lessons. See, I've been so tired at night because I'm just getting used to the hot sun, but now I'm ready to start, because—"

"Hold on, don't give me a sermon. You are ready to start?"

"Yes, ma'am."

"That's good," Miss Elmilly said.

"Jesse," Aunt May inquired, "are you giving Miss Elmilly any trouble?"

They smiled.

"I reckon you'll have to ask her that."

"I see. Do you like the sawmill?"

"Yes, ma'am. I like the lumber when it comes out. But the mill's so *loud*, that's the only thing."

"Put something in your ears," Miss Elmilly said. "Didn't Will Evans give you something?"

"Yes, ma'am."

"Well, wear it, for heaven's sake!"

"I will."

They sat there on the porch, chatting and content, until Jesse barely heard them. His eyes closed.

"Look at him," Miss Elmilly said. "That's what I mean about too tired to study."

"I'm okay," he said sleepily.

"And I've got to go," Aunt May said.

She stood up and Jesse shook himself saying he'd like to walk her down the street. The sun was already down.

"Hurry back, now," Miss Elmilly said, "I'm not keeping your supper warm all night."

"Yes ma'am, I will."

Then he was finally alone with his aunt.

"Paw was here today," he said. "He followed me to the swimming hole."

"What did he say? Did he want your pay from the mill?"

"Yes."

"He's been talking about it when he gets drunk. You hide it good and watch for him."

"I will. Listen, Aunt May, I need to ask you some things."

She looked sideways at him.

"Did you help him with the dead fish? He said you did."

She was silent and Jesse could hear their footsteps on the hard gravel road.

"Yes, honey, I did that."

They walked on and he heard a dog bark, and the soft calling of a barred owl, and their steps again. The sky was dark blue. He didn't know what to say.

"He was coming to get you, to help him. Said he couldn't do it alone."

"I wouldn't go! Listen, I've changed a lot, Aunt May. I've decided—"

"Hold on, Jesse. I'm glad to hear it. But I just wanted to save you the trouble he'd cause. I know how you feel about the fish."

"I wish we could stop him."

"I do too." She walked along thinking. "We could, I guess. I could turn the old dog in."

"Put him in prison?"

"Sure could. I'm the one could do it. But do you think I ought to?"

"I don't know."

"Think of this: one day he'd get out again. What would happen to all of us then? What would happen to May that night? It'd be my last hour on earth, wouldn't it?"

"Yes, ma'am."

"It sure would."

"Well, I don't want you doing it just to protect me."

"Don't worry about that. You won't be young long. Let me help out while I still can."

The deep purple sky turned to black and the stars became bright. There was a wide low orange moon in the trees.

"Aunt May, tell me the truth about how Mama died."

"The truth? She got sick."

"And went swimming?"

"Swimming? That's ridiculous. Who told you that?"

"Paw. He said she went swimming in Bluebottom Creek and drowned. She was sick and out of her head."

"Oh."

"Well," Jesse said edgily, "what about it, Aunt May?"

"She wasn't swimming. She went walking, wandering. She was out of her head I guess."

"And she just fell in the creek?"

"I wasn't here! Nobody was. Your paw found her right after it happened. Jesse, don't think about this thing! It won't do any of us any good."

"Paw said she went swimming."

"Well, I don't know. Maybe he thought she did."

"Was that possible?"

"I suppose it was."

"It's a long, long way to that tressel, Aunt May. How could she walk there out of her head?"

"Well, she was upset, had a fever. She wasn't crazy or anything."

"Upset?"

"Jesse *please* don't question me!"

"You say she might have been swimming then, but she wasn't crazy."

Aunt May put her palms on his face. Finally she raised them and said, "That's right. I guess that's right."

"No, it's not right," Jesse said in a determined level voice. "Because Robert Elmer told me it was a big flood. You have to remember that, too."

"Oh, yes, I do, because he had a time getting her body from it."

"So she couldn't have been swimming unless she was out of her mind, Aunt May. Nobody swims in a flood."

"Oh."

"Just, 'oh?' "

"I told you I wasn't there, Jesse! Nobody was!"

"I think somebody was, all right," he said, turning on the dark road. "I'm pretty sure somebody was."

He walked on alone and said out loud to himself: "She didn't just die. He killed her. I know she didn't just die."

Chapter 10

The next afternoon Jesse took a long walk after work.
He came in at dark and was in the bathtub soaping
up his arms, when Miss Elmilly yelled through the
door: "Your brothers said they'd be by at eight thirty
to pick you up, and they said to be ready."

"What on earth for?"

"They didn't say, but they were in a mighty good
mood."

"I see."

"Well, I'll have your supper ready, Jesse, soon as
you get your bath."

At eight thirty they pulled up in a loud ramshackle
pickup that had once been painted blue

"Come on, boy!" Bean yelled. "Let's go!"

"What's this about?" he said.

"Don't worry," Bean confided with a grin. "It's too
secret to go blabbin about. You'll be glad you come!"
He winked in Jesse's face.

"Does this have anything to do with Paw?"

"He don't know a thing about it," Bean said.

He got into the pickup truck and they roared away, embarrassing him with the rattle of their rotten muffler. They were both in high spirits, and Bean drove while Robert Elmer passed a fruit jar of moonshine between them. Jesse was in the middle and he was already sorry he'd come.

"Where'd you get the truck?" he asked.

"Bought it," Bean said happily, "for a hundred dollars."

They reached the highway and turned west, and Bean pushed the old Chevy up to sixty-five.

"Aren't you afraid of the law?" Jesse asked.

"Listen to this boy's proper speech!" Bean laughed. "That old lady been *workin* on him!"

"I hear him," Robert Elmer said, smiling.

"We been leavin you out of things," Bean said. "And we just realized it. You ain't no baby brother no more. Just *look* at your ass!"

Jesse looked at his legs, his arms.

"You gettin *size* on you, boy," Robert Elmer said. "Me and Bean got to thinkin, here you be growed up in a minute, and we leavin you out."

Jesse hoped they'd keep *on* leaving him out of things.

"We takin you to our club," Bean grinned, raising the fruit jar. "You might say."

"You're in a club?"

"Damn right," Robert Elmer said. "Every decent boy in the county ought to be in it, too."

"To tell you the truth," Bean said, "we ain't exactly thought of you ourselves. Robert Elmer, he's been eat up with chasin that there *Gloria.*" Bean looked over at his brother and grinned.

They sped on into the colors of the sunset.

"But, what I'm gettin to," Bean went on, "one of the fellas in the club pointed it out to us—here they is, spendin time and money tryin to get all these boys in the high schools to join—and we got us a little brother the right age, sittin underneath our noses."

"Hell yes," Robert Elmer said grimly.

"Them high school boys join up right and left, too," Bean said. "You need some buddies, Jess. You spend too much time by yourself."

"Want some?" Robert Elmer asked, offering the jar.

"No thanks. Where are we going?"

"Well, there's three kinds of meetins in the club. Secret ones, ones what are open to all the members, and public meetins like tonight, where *anybody* can come."

"It's a showin of strength," Robert Elmer said.

"Ain't nobody supposed to know who we are, though," Bean said, "so we got *disguises. Great* disguises. Wait till you see em."

"Bean," Jesse said, "what are you talking about?"

"The Ku Klux Klan, Jesse boy. The old KKK. And we are gonna propose your name for membership just as soon as you give the word."

"You know that boy that was botherin you at work?" Robert Elmer said.

"Who, Nathan?"

"That's the one. Well, me and Bean and a couple of boys from the klavern might just pay him a little visit."

"What do you mean?"

"Break some of his windows, scare him. *That's* the kind of work we do. And let me tell you, boy, there's a plenty of it to be done."

Jesse felt sick.

"You ain't kiddin," Robert Elmer said seriously, as if he were contemplating the vast evil in the world.

"You see, little brother," Bean said, "the Klan was formed back at the end of the Civil War to keep the freed slaves down. And you don't know this, but if they hadn't done it, *all these years*, things would be a hell of a lot worse."

"Amen," Robert Elmer said.

"But there's plenty of problems," Bean said. "Like blacks and whites swimmin together at the community center."

"It's done got clean out of hand," Robert Elmer said.

"It's to the point now," Bean said, "that the young white kids think there ain't nothin wrong with it. They think it's just splashin and playin in water."

"Fools," Robert Elmer said.

"But look here," Bean said, "they in the schools, now they in the swimmin pools. Next thing they be *marryin* some weak-minded cracker."

"Zebras," Robert Elmer said.

"Polka-dots," Bean said. "It's bein rammed down

our throats by the Yankees. They been mixed up so long, until they don't even *know* the difference."

"I'm gonna tell you what," Robert Elmer said very seriously, looking Jesse in the face and breathing his whiskey breath, "it's time to draw the line."

"And that's where the Klan comes in," Bean said with a grin. "And *you* can be a part of it!"

He turned off the highway into a big field. There were lots of cars and pickup trucks parked there, and Bean drove to the edge of the lot and stopped.

They got out and Robert Elmer reached behind the seat.

"This here's for you," he said.

His arms were full of wrinkled white sheets. He handed Jesse one.

"Got your knife?" Bean asked.

"Yeah."

"Well, cut yourself some eye holes. I didn't know where to put em."

He and Robert Elmer pulled their sheets over their heads. They looked at him through ragged eye holes.

"I don't want to wear this thing," Jesse said.

"The hell you say," Robert Elmer said. Bean stepped between them.

"Look," Bean said, "the idea is, *they* won't know who we are. We could be *anybody*. But if you show your face, they'll figure me and Robert Elmer must be here."

"*They* are going to be here?"

"Well naw, but white folks who ain't members might be."

"But *I'm* not a member."

"Just do it," Robert Elmer said. "I ain't gonna ask you again."

Jesse took his sheet and cut the eye holes. He pulled it over his head and followed through the parked cars and trucks. He felt ridiculous.

They approached the crowd of white-sheeted people and Jesse saw a stage erected in the center, and behind it a huge wooden cross.

A sheeted man stepped onto the stage and a microphone was passed up to him.

"Praise the Lord!" he shouted.

"Praise the Lord!" the crowd replied.

"Let thy light shine, said Jesus!" he yelled. "Let it be *seen* on this earth!"

With those words, a torch was lit to the cross. Jesse thought it must have been soaked with gasoline, because the fire ran straight up it and out the arms.

"I want all the young folks to see this," he said in an emotional preacher-voice, "this here's the symbol of white Christian purity!"

"Amen, brother," from the crowd.

"*Purity*, I said! In a time of unbelief!

"Purity! In the face of yankee supreme court devilment!

"Purity! When Mexicans are comin over the Texas border every day, every single day, to take jobs away from Americans!

"Purity, I said! When black faces walk the hallways of our schools and colleges!"

He paused and gripped his microphone stand tightly through his sheet. He seemed to stagger.

"Amen, brother!" from the crowd.

"But ohhhhhhh," the man on the stage said with more gravel in his voice, "it does my heart good to see y'all here tonight!"

"All right!" someone next to Jesse shouted.

"There's a curse upon this fine land," he said. "Puerto *Ricans* swarmin in the northern cities! Portu-*guese* swarmin up and down the coast of New England! And ever single President we get appoints another judge with a black face!"

"Tell it!" someone yelled.

"It's the truth, brothers and sisters!"

Sisters? Jesse looked around. Were there women here?

"But the tide is going to turn. It's got to or America is done for. I know that for a fact and you do, too. And ever day more and more young people is *joinin* our rolls, hot *dog!*"

"Hot dog!" from the crowd.

"You travel up and down this land of ours," he said with his voice rasping, "you travel as I have done, and you will see hundreds and hundreds of fine white Christian churches!"

His voice broke with a tear and the crowd went up in shouts of, "Amen! Tell it, brother!"

"White Christian womanhood, let me tell you!"

"Say it!"

"Young girls, oh Lord to mercy, with smooth pink skin!"

"Lord Jesus!"

"Growin up to become fine Christian mothers!"

"All right!"

"Mothers with white girls of their *own* to raise up!"

"Don't you *know!*"

"And I don't know about you," he said in a furious, frantic voice, "but I don't ever want to see a black boy lookin at one of them girls again!"

"No! No!" the crowd screamed. "Lord no!"

"Now, I want to see you in your churches."

"Yes sir, amen!"

"And I want you to pray for this racial situation."

"That's right."

"But I'm standin here before you right now," he paused and seemed about to cry, "to tell you, folks, that just ain't *enough!*"

"No! It ain't enough."

"No, sir and no, ma'am, it just ain't enough. The Lord said He helps them what helps *themselves*, now ain't that what He said?"

"That's right! That's what He said!"

"So I'm here to tell you, we got to help ourselves, we got to *act!* And when a brother speaks to you about joinin the Ku Klux Klan, that's when I want you to *act!*"

"Yes sir, brother! Amen to that! The Ku Klux Klan!" The crowd was cheering and Jesse could hear men and women moaning behind the sheets.

"That's the message, folks. You know it's right! Now if you want to join tonight, just step down here to the foot of this podium, and we'll flat sign you up. We also have some inspirational long-playing records up here, and full glossy photographs of Andrew Young drinkin coffee with communists."

Bean elbowed Jesse in the ribs.

"You wanta join?" he asked.

Jesse stared at him. He looked the other way and saw Robert Elmer looming over him, listening for his answer.

"Uh, I reckon I'll think it over," he said.

"Sure," Bean said. "But boy, if *that* speech didn't do it to you, I don't know what would."

They got into the pickup and roared down the highway. Jesse felt good to be out from under the hot sheet.

"Gimme that jar," Bean said.

"Well, looky here," Robert Elmer said, "it's empty."

"Ain't there another one?"

Robert Elmer reached his long arms under the truck seat and felt around, finally coming up with one.

"All right!" Bean said. "Put the pedal to the metal!"

The truck rattled through town and came to a halt outside Miss Elmilly's. Jesse slammed the door and walked up the lane without telling them goodnight.

Chapter 11

Jesse learned from Nathan that the Evans' house was just north of town, in a grove of pine trees beside a lake.

He went to the town barber Saturday morning, lay back in the chair and gazed at photographs of young men with blown-dry hair cuts and movie-star grins. On the street he had seen a few high school boys with styles like that. Then he closed his eyes while the old barber worked, combing Jesse's blond hair furiously. He talked about World War II, a time when men were proud of short hair. Then he told Jesse about the sixties, when a lot of boys were cowards and wore their hair long to prove it.

It was a bad time, he said, for barbers.

When he was finished, Jesse stared at himself in the wall mirror, not believing what he saw. He looked like one of the photographs.

He also couldn't believe it when the man charged him three dollars.

As he walked toward the pine grove, Jesse thought

about the town. He was used to the place in a strange way. But he didn't know many people, and so far it seemed Bean was partly right: they weren't in any hurry to make friends with a Watersmith.

That was all right. They didn't give him any trouble, either. He heard mutterings about Robert Elmer, but that was his own doing. He had thought he might talk too much like a country hick, and town folks might laugh at him. But he couldn't hear any difference in his speech from theirs. If anything, the habits he'd picked up from Aunt May were a little better than a lot of the town people. So all he felt he was really missing was whatever they knew from school. And so far, working with Miss Elmilly from the old textbooks, he wasn't hitting anything too hard.

He knew, from the conversation overheard on Miss Elmilly's porch, that Aunt May thought he was smart. And it amazed him how confident that made him feel as he attacked the schoolbooks. He was up to the junior high books already, in just a few days. And they had been wrong about one thing. There was one book in camp that he had read, or at least parts. The Bible. It was the only thing *to* read, and because he hadn't had anybody to interpret it for him, he had an unusual understanding of it. He knew a lot of the stories by heart, and a lot of ideas passed through his mind like leaves before the wind, without a pattern.

Then he was on the trail from the Evans mailbox, down through the thick pines, and he heard a dog barking, and laughter.

Mr. Evans and Ren were tossing a white Frisbee and a big Irish setter was jumping up between them, trying to intercept it.

Ren saw him and sailed it toward him, flat and even, straight to his chest and he grabbed it out of the air.

"Good!" Mr. Evans cried.

But when he tried to sail it to Mr. Evans he watched miserably as it went off into the trees.

Ren was laughing and the dog got it and ran around the house.

"That's all right," Mr. Evans said, walking up and offering his hand. "I was about tired out anyway."

Jesse smiled and shook his hand.

"This is my daughter Ren," he said.

"Hello," Jesse said.

She had a wide beautiful face, with the same light gray eyes as her father, and lots of freckles.

"She's the same age as you."

"Hello, Jesse," she said.

She stood with a relaxed dignity he had never seen. She tossed back her hair slightly and smiled at him.

He felt his face flush.

"I believe lunch is ready for us," Mr. Evans said, "come on this way."

He followed them in.

The room had a wall of windows, looking out on the still lake. They stood on a thick, dark green carpet, before a glass-topped table set and loaded with hot vegetables and a ham. The air-conditioned room was full of white wicker furniture.

An energetic plump lady came from around the kitchen counter, which was all that separated the two rooms.

"I'm Mrs. Evans," she said, taking his hand in both of hers. "We're mightly pleased to have you here today."

"Thank you, ma'am."

"Getting cold!" Mr. Evans said. "Let's sit down!"

They did, and Jesse followed their example in bowing his head and closing his eyes.

Mr. Evans thanked Jesus for the food and the house and the company.

Jesse watched how they held their knives and forks. It didn't seem unusual but he just knew he'd stumble over something soon.

The hot butterbeans melted in his mouth.

"You sure can cook," he said right away.

They all laughed.

"Thank you so much," she said. Mrs. Evans was a pretty, roundish woman with streaks of gray in her brown hair. Her eyes were deep brown and had an expression both warm and timid.

"Do you eat well where you're staying?" Mr. Evans asked.

"Oh, yes. Miss Elmilly can cook like Aunt May."

"Aunt May?"

"My mother's sister. She lives with us."

"I see. Is there anybody else up in that camp?"

"Uh, no sir, just me and my brothers."

"And your father."

"Yes."

"Is it true you never went to school?" Ren asked.

"Yes, it is."

"Lucky!"

"Ren!" her mother said. "We don't know how Jesse feels about it. Maybe he'd rather go to school!"

"Well, let's ask him," Mr. Evans said, smiling. "How about it, Jesse?"

He looked at them as he chewed a mouthful of cornbread and butterbeans.

"I guess the truth is, I don't know what I'm missing."

The answer seemed to impress them.

"Well, *I* do," Ren said carelessly, "you're missing a lot of slobs and boneheads and stuffed animals for teachers."

He laughed but Mrs. Evans said, "Renly Anne!" sharply.

Jesse enjoyed the meal of thinly sliced ham and fresh new potatoes with cream sauce, and all the rest.

When they got to the dessert of homemade boiled custard ice cream he thought he would burst.

Finally Mrs. Evans and Ren carried off the dishes while Mr. Evans slowly packed his briar pipe and lit it, and Jesse sat watching the beautiful motionless lake through the wall of windows.

When Ren rejoined them she was quiet and expectant, as if waiting for something that was going to happen.

"Jesse," Mr. Evans finally said, "I'd still like to hear about growing up in the swamp. You said you'd tell me."

"Yes, sir, I guess I did. I don't know exactly what to say, though."

"Well, let me see. You seem at ease here, so I'd guess you came to town as a boy. Am I right?"

"Yes. Aunt May brought me some. I don't know much about town, but I'm not a wild animal, if that's what you mean."

Jesse couldn't believe he'd said this: but it seemed the thing to say.

"No," Mr. Evans said very coolly, "you don't seem to be."

"I just mean, I'm no different from anybody else, really."

"I'm sure you're not. You must love the woods, and know them well, is that true?"

"Yes. Paw does, too, and he taught me."

"I know he does. He used to be on my timber cutting crew just like he is now. He could take one look at an aerial map or a courthouse description of a piece of property, and lead my men right to it. Smart as he could be. And a fast man with a chain saw."

"But you fired him before."

Mr. Evans looked calmly at Jesse. "Yes, I had to. Your father's problem isn't his work. His work is usually top notch. It's the trouble he gets himself into."

"Did he burn down a . . . a man's house?"

"The Ku Klux Klan did it. He was the only one who lost his hood in the wind and got recognized."

Jesse felt his face turn hot.

"It was back when a lot of college kids were coming

here trying to register black voters. The rednecks were stirred up like rattlesnakes against them. Nathan Brown had a skinny little blond girl staying with him and his wife. She was a slip of a thing, but she wasn't afraid of anybody, or, at least, not that she showed."

"She lived there?"

"For a while. Until the house got burned to the ground. When all that stuff happened, Jesse, you just can't imagine how hot feelings ran around here. It looks a little different to me now. But at the time I was mad myself. Only I didn't hold with killing or burning to make the point."

"How does it look different?" Jesse asked.

"Well, I can see some good that's come. Blacks aren't as scared as they used to be. More of them vote."

"But," Ren said, "they still don't have good jobs."

"That's true. It's worse, of course, in areas where you have so many unskilled people. But it's not just blacks who suffer, Jesse. The South is full of poor white folks that don't have jobs either, or they have some little job that just gets them by. Now, to *their* way of seeing, the person threatening to steal that miserable job is a black person. Do you get me?"

"I think so."

"That's the reason they hate them so much, really. It goes back to the times of slavery. And they have all these so-called leaders that whip them up about it."

"The Ku Klux Klan?"

"Yes, and the Nazi Party, of all things. Jesse, did

you know those organizations even get into the high schools and recruit young boys?"

"No, sir."

"Well, they do. Actually, there's a lot of evidence things may be getting worse. The Klan seems to be making a comeback."

"I can feel it at school," Ren said.

"How is that?" Jesse asked.

"Well, the black kids keep to themselves more than they used to. And if you talk to one a few days in a row some of the whites start to make fun of you."

"Oh."

"It's disgusting," she said. "I can't wait to move to Virginia."

"We'll see about that," Mr. Evans said. "The part of Virginia where you want to go doesn't have many blacks. But if it did, you'd see the same problems."

"Maybe," she said. "There's nothing I can do about it anyway."

"That's the sad part," Mr. Evans said to Jesse. "I can't hire any more people than I already work, and I surely can't pay them more. I just bought a big track of timber from Sheriff Riggins' mother. That's the only reason I could hire you Watersmiths. But that strained it to the limit. There are too many people in this world for the jobs, and television has made them lazy. They all have a TV set, and they all lie there week after week watching rich people in fast, gas-guzzling cars race up and down the freeways in cities. They think that looks better than spending the rest of their lives slapping mosquitoes and trying to grow corn in a red clay garden."

"It is better," Ren said.

"No," Mr. Evans answered. "It's not. But it would take a person who'd already experienced both to understand."

"Like you?" Ren said.

The moment hung between them.

Jesse was embarrassed.

Then Mr. Evans put the fingers of both hands on the table's edge and said very gently, "Maybe I'm wrong. I don't know it all. But I know one thing: people had better start expecting less of the material things of life, and think more on the spiritual blessings. Because the world just ain't set up to make everybody rich, or even half-rich."

"Expect less?" Ren said. "That's your solution?"

"I know I might feel differently if I were down in shanty town, drinking rotgut, and my wife was somebody's maid."

"*Might?*" Ren cried.

"Oh, all right, I would feel differently. If I were there, instead of here, there'd be ten or so less jobs in this world. I keep eight family men working, you know."

"I know, Daddy," she said, suddenly reaching out and covering his hand with her own. "I'm sorry I sounded mean."

"You didn't, honey. You know, we've gotten *way* off the track! I still want to hear about growing up in the woods!"

Jesse smiled. "Well, one thing I'll tell you. You don't hear any talk like this out there."

They all laughed as Mrs. Evans flowed into the

room wearing a light blue dress that rustled loudly when she moved, and sparkling jewelry.

"I'm off to the church," she said. "I've made three flower arrangements for tomorrow's service, and I need some help carrying them to the car."

Jesse and Ren and Mr. Evans each carried one. They were heavy and quite beautiful. They positioned them carefully in the back seat.

"Want somebody to ride with you and unload?" Mr. Evans asked.

"No thanks," she said sweetly, "the preacher promised to meet me there with his maid."

"All right then."

She drove slowly away.

"I've got to make a few business calls," Mr. Evans said. "Ren, why don't you show Jesse around the place?"

"Okay."

"Good. Jesse, make yourself at home now."

"Yes, sir," he said. "I sure will."

Chapter 12

They walked beside the lake and the sun was hot.

"Mother works so hard for that church," she said. "And it drives her crazy."

"It does?"

"Yes. She's real good at flower arrangements. She's got lots of books on it. And the preacher has this wife . . ." Ren rolled her eyes and smiled. "She *means* well, but she has no sense of balance. Like she'll breeze into the vestibule, take a quick look, and move a few stems around."

"And that ruins it?"

"Oh yes. For instance, you always use uneven numbers to stand out: three major flowers, or five . . . see?"

"I guess."

"Well, try putting two or four up sometime, each with equal weight in the arrangement, and you'll see what I mean."

Jesse nodded. He tried to imagine arranging flowers.

"Look!" Jesse said.

He pointed to the lake. A big bullfrog sat on one side of a long finger of land, and a snake was swimming toward him from the other side.

Jesse picked up a flat rock, drew back, and skipped it across the water toward them. The frog jumped and the snake submerged.

"Good throw," she said.

Ren looked at Jesse and they both smiled.

"What are the kids here like?"

"By the age of fourteen," she said, "the boys all dip snuff and chew tobacco. They're into putting goats in the school bathroom, stuff like that."

He laughed. "What about the girls?"

"I have the most trouble with them. They resent me, I think, because I talk a little like Virginia. Do you hear it?"

"Is that what it is?"

"Yes." She smiled with him. "That's what it is. At first I used to practice it to make myself sound better than them. Now I don't care to do that, but I can't help it."

"I can understand that," he said seriously.

"I used to beg Mother and Daddy to let me go to a private school in New Hampshire, but they wouldn't. They said I was all they had and they couldn't do without me."

Jesse looked at her, trying to imagine what it would be like to have such parents.

"I don't care so much now," she said, kicking a rock, "I'm just waiting it out. I don't need them."

"Who?"

"The kids."

"Oh, yeah."

"They're all going to stay here all their lives, and I'm leaving as soon as I'm eighteen, and that's just the way it is."

"Where will you go?"

Jesse felt suddenly sad, left behind, even though he had just met her.

"Virginia. And New York City. I want to live in both places but finally I want to settle in Virginia and raise horses with my grandparents."

"I wish I knew everything I want to do, like you."

"Oh, I don't know so much!" She laughed a little bitterly. "Mainly I know where I *don't* want to live: right here. I want to go to college and then travel for a while."

They kept walking slowly around the lake. At the far end there was a small stable. Jesse smelled the pleasant aroma of horse.

"Come here," Ren said.

The gray dappled mare he had first seen her riding stuck her head out of the stall and snorted.

"Her name is Raffasha," Ren said, smoothing the horse's face. "She has royal blood."

"Royal blood?"

"Yes. She's desert-bred. I have her lineage traced back *hundreds* of years. I could talk about Arabians all day, Jesse."

"Are these what your grandparents raise?"

"Yes. They gave her to me. I'm going to breed her next year."

Ren opened a clean metal garbage can and it was

full of grain. She scooped some out and poured it into a bucket hung inside the stall. Then she unlatched the door and swung it open.

"She needs to walk a little. I'll take her for a long ride when it cools off this evening."

"She's mighty pretty."

"You're not kidding. She's going to be the beginning of my own herd."

His eyes widened as he looked at her and at the horse. She was so confident.

"Do you ride?" she asked.

"No, I never have. Except once I remember Paw put me on a mule somewhere. It was fine until we were heading back to the barn, and the mule started to run. I got scared and started crying and almost fell off. That mule tore into the barn with me hanging from his neck."

She laughed with him.

"I hope that didn't turn you against horses."

"No."

"Want to ride with me some time? I could teach you."

"Sure. But what horse would I ride?"

"I'll see what I can do. Daddy can borrow one, I'm sure. Course it won't be anything like Raffasha."

"Course. You must love this place," he said, gazing around.

"I grew up with it. I know I take it for granted. Someday I'll probably look back and appreciate it, but right now I can't wait to escape."

"That's how I feel."

"You want to escape?"

"Not from the woods. But from my father, and my brothers."

"What does he do?"

"He used to whip us a lot. He gets drunk and hits my aunt."

"He wouldn't hit me but once," she declared.

"Well . . ."

"Well, what? When's the last time he hit you?"

"Aw, a few months ago. I'm getting too big now, and he knows it."

"That's horrible, Jesse. Your mother's dead?"

"Yes."

"You poor thing."

He shrugged his shoulders, feeling uncomfortable with sympathy.

"So you want to escape?"

"Yes. If I had a place to go like you do, I'd take off today."

"You have nobody to go to at all?"

"No."

"What about your aunt?"

"I can't leave without her. Someday I'll take her off with me."

"She lives up in the woods?"

"Yes. We each have our own tent. Paw stays in the trailer he had when Mama was still alive."

Jesse's mouth grew tight and his voice became hard and flat. They were silent for a moment.

"You hate him?"

"Yes," he whispered. "I hate him."

"That's awful," she whispered to him. "Just awful."

He started walking and they followed the oval shoreline of the lake.

"So your daddy wouldn't let you leave?" he asked.

"No indeed. Part of it was that he doesn't approve of his in-laws. He likes them, but he objects to their wealthy style."

Jesse looked puzzled.

"You see, they inherited money, and land. They've had time to read, study music, travel to Europe, things like that. Daddy came up the hard way and he believes in work, work, work."

"He likes his sawmill, doesn't he?"

"He loves it. He grew up around his father's little mill. Now *Mother*, she's a character. She's very proud of being in the DAR. Know that?"

"No."

"Daughters of the American Revolution. You have to trace your ancestors back that far. Mother never has been comfortable really, living down here. But once in a while she goes back and visits her folks for a week, and realizes *this* is her home."

They walked in silence again.

They finally came to the house.

Mr. Evans was standing under the pines smoking his pipe. Jesse smelled it before he saw him.

"You get the tour?"

"Yes, sir. It's beautiful here."

"Thank you."

The big red dog came up and rubbed against Ren.

"Guess I better go," Jesse said. "Thanks for having me over."

"You're more than welcome," Mr. Evans said.

"I'll walk you out to the road," Ren said.

"Well," Jesse said awkwardly to Mr. Evans, "so long. See you Monday."

"Fine."

They came to the mailbox at the beginning of the drive.

The dog nudged between them jealously.

"Want to go riding next Saturday?" she asked without looking straight at him.

"Sure."

"Okay. I'll see if I can get you a horse."

"Sounds great."

"Come early. Is seven in the morning all right?"

"Sure, I'll be here."

"Just come down to the stable. If I can't get you a horse, I'll let you know during the week."

"Okay, Ren."

"Bye," she said.

She ran back down the drive with the dog jumping ahead of her, his body twisting from side to side.

Chapter 13

Jesse never knew time to crawl by as slowly as it did the next week. He was afraid Ren would show up with bad news about borrowing him a horse, but Thursday came and she hadn't yet. That day Nathan shied away from Jesse at the mill, and acted like he didn't want to talk. Jesse followed him as he started to walk home at the end of the day.

"Nathan," he said, "wait. Can I walk with—"

"No!" he said, looking about. "You best leave me alone, young man."

Jesse followed Nathan's gaze and searched the men, breaking up and drifting from the mill. His brothers stood and watched.

"It's them, isn't it? What did they say to you?"

"Listen!" Nathan said hurriedly. "If you got to talk to me, slip down to my house tonight after dark. *Alone*, you hear? By yo *self*."

"But where do you—"

Nathan turned and walked quickly away from him. Who can I ask? he wondered. Then Jesse turned and walked alone toward Miss Elmilly's.

That night he worked hard at his lessons and finished them by nine o'clock. There was just a faint glow on the western side of the sky as he walked past the humble storefronts of the town and down into the black section. The paintless, ramshackle houses twisted this way and that under the slow power of the shifting earth beneath them. They had only wooden foundations that moved with the mud.

Suddenly a fluffy red thing, faster than a dog, shot out from under one of the shacks and stood facing him. He couldn't believe he was looking at a fox.

"You're Nathan's fox!" he cried.

"Thas right, boy," the old man said from the shadows of his yard. "I see you found the way."

The fox sniffed and darted around him.

He sat down on his heels and petted it.

"So this is where you live," Jesse said.

"This it. I will invite you in if you willin."

"What do you mean?"

"Look yonder," Nathan said, pointing at his front windows. One of them was a square of yellow light, the other a patch of taped cardboard.

"You know who done that?"

"No."

"Them brothers of yours. Watersmiths done that."

"Why?"

"That there was their way of tellin me to leave you alone."

"Those sorry—what did they say to you?"

"Calm down, now. They come by here, insultin my wife, insultin me. They found my boy drunk, and that got em on fire. 'Just like one,' thas what they said."

"I'm sorry, Nathan. They're crazy."

"Wasn't none of your fault. Now look here. I coulda gone to Mr. Evans and I believe he would put them back on the road. I don't believe *that* man would have old Nathan treated so."

"I'm glad you didn't. I would have had to quit, too. And go back to the swamp."

"Hm hmmm. I see. Well now, sometime a man's family can be a stone around his neck. A stone around him, thas what."

The screen door opened and a heavy, slow-moving black woman appeared on the slanting porch. She wore loose flowing clothes and seemed to be dragging something.

"Who's that?" she said.

"Who you *think?*" Nathan snapped. "Come on in if you want to, boy. I ain't afraid."

"Thank you, sir," Jesse said.

Nathan gave him a quick stare. They both knew that nothing would make the brothers any madder than to hear that. And it made them both uncomfortable.

"This that little Watersmith boy I was tellin you bout," Nathan said, leading the way in.

His hand was raised in the air as if to ask her not to yell.

"He's a good boy, Roxanne. He can't help his folks."

"Well *I* ain't blockin the door," she said. "I been wantin to see him anyway."

Nathan stopped and looked quickly at both of them, then led the way again up the rotten steps.

Jesse wondered why on earth this woman wanted to see him. Especially when it could get his brothers after them.

He stopped on the porch and looked around. There was a single dead tree in the little dirt yard, with all its branches cut off to a length of two feet. It was whitewashed and stuck on the end of each branch was a blue jug.

The small living room had a comfortable but gloomy feeling. Old furniture that looked beaten to death by children long ago was carefully arranged around a coffee table. The walls had once been covered with a now-faded flowery wallpaper, and the lines of each weathered board showed through. Dim bulbs in the two lamps gave a solemn yellowish cast to things.

Roxanne and Nathan didn't stop there. They kept going and Jesse followed them to the kitchen in back. Here a brighter lamp sat on the formica table.

Roxanne served them iced tea.

"So you Jesse," she finally said as she settled her bulk into a small chair. "You don't look like you bite."

"Hush!" Nathan said. "I told you he was all right."

"I know what you told me," she said, leaning over slightly and peering into Jesse's face.

She had bright black eyes, and her face was still smooth and pretty in spite of the age and weight.

"I know everything you said," Roxanne went on, not looking at Nathan. "But I can't take no chance.

Boy, if you tell a living soul you been here, them night riders will come burn us down."

"I won't," Jesse said. "I really won't."

"Well," she said, "just remember that it mean a lot more to me than it do to you."

"I will."

They heard a clatter in the back yard.

"Thas Charlie," Nathan said. "He the last one of our chillen lef to home. He the only one that dropped off."

"Dropped off?" Jessie asked.

"Thas right, he—"

The back door swung open and slammed against the counter.

"Hello, Ma," he slurred. "Oh ho!" He saw Jesse and seemed to hang suspended for a moment, neither standing nor leaning. "What kind of company is this?"

"Don't trouble yo self," Nathan said, "this a hard working boy from the mill."

Roxanne scowled at Charlie.

"I bet he is," Charlie said, staggering over to Jesse and glaring down into his face. He was a big man with scars across his nose, and he smelled of whiskey.

"What yo name, boy?" Charlie asked.

"Jesse Watersmith," he said, a little angrily.

"One them Watersmiths that come in here?"

"Yes, but—"

"One them that runs that *whiskey*." He grinned with his broken teeth into Jesse's face.

"Yeah," Jesse said.

"You come down to shanty town to sell whiskey?"

"No he did not!" Nathan roared. His small head and tightly muscled neck stuck out over the bright table like an angry turtle.

"I had some yo whiskey," Charlie said, trying to ignore his father.

"The boy ain't part of that," Nathan said. "Now if you don't mind I would like for you to leave our company."

"Watersmith whiskey," Charlie said, looking at the ceiling. He shambled from the room. "Yeah," he mumbled, "I had some of that."

"That there," Nathan said, "what I call 'dropped off.' The whiskey bottle got him. Charlie was a good boy one time, but he ain't been much fo bout the last five years."

"I'm sorry," Jesse said.

"Oh? Well, ain't *yo* sorrow. You got yo own, anyway."

"Jesse," Roxanne said, "do you love Jesus?"

He had never been asked such a thing.

"I . . . don't know."

"Don't know? Does you read the Bible?"

"Yes. Sometimes."

"Well, does you believe what the Bible says?"

"Uh, yes. I reckon."

"He reckon." Roxanne looked at Nathan, exasperated.

"He been livin back up in them *swamps*, woman. What you expect?" Nathan said.

"Well, here's the thing I'm comin to. Does you remember where Jesus went up on the mountain and spoke to the spirits of Abraham and Moses?"

"I remember that."

"Thas good. Now, you know, when that happened, them men had been dead a *long* time."

"Yes, ma'am."

Roxanne hesitated but went on.

"But Jesus was still able to talk with them. Now, you ever heard of such a thing happenin in the present day?"

"No, ma'am."

"But ain't any reason why it shouldn't. Thas right?"

"That's right, I guess."

"I don't know . . ." Nathan said.

"Husband it's my *duty*."

"All right, all right."

"Now Jesse, there's some folks in the world today who, by the power of the Lord Jesus Christ, is able to talk with dead spirits."

Jesse couldn't say anything to that.

"Only they ain't *dead*."

She got up and walked to the refrigerator. She limped, and moved heavily but with a gracefulness. The backs of her arms were enormous.

After she refilled the iced tea glasses and resettled herself in the little chair, she looked Jesse in the eye.

"Sometimes Jesus lets *me* talk with them spirits. I don't say nothing, but I go into a little sleep, and them spirits speak through me."

"What do they say?" Jesse asked.

"Nathan writes it all down," she said. "I don't even hear it, and I don't remember one word."

"Mostly she gets messages from Jesus about our friends," Nathan said. "He tells if they are sick, or *goin* to be sick, and what they better do."

"It's a holy work," Roxanne said. "It don't come from *me*, it come from Him."

"That's great," Jesse said.

"Yes," she said, "it be great that the Lord chose me for such a task. But son, once in a while I get another type of message. Somebody over there wants to send a little advice or somethin to somebody over here."

"They do?"

"Yes Jesse, they *do*. What I'm tryin to tell you, is I keep gettin yo name. Somebody wants to tell you somethin."

"*My* name? Who on earth is it?"

"It ain't *on* earth, exactly. It's somebody by the name of Tanya."

Jesse felt weak. His throat went dry and his hands were sweating as he held onto the edge of the table.

"Do that mean something to you?" Roxanne asked.

"Yes," Jesse breathed.

"Someone close to you, who died?"

"Yes. She was my mother." He could barely speak.

"Mercy," Roxanne said. "Well, three times she asked bout you. She ain't said much because of some problem."

"What do you mean?"

"Could be anything. She ain't learned to do it right yet; or somethin's troublin her and she don't know

jus exactly what she wants to say. You can't tell.
How long since she done passed over?"

"Uh. Twelve years."

"Well, whatever it is, she sho got you on her mind.
She done tried three times but all she said was, first,
yo name, then *her* name, then she say 'You must
hurry, you must hurry,' and then, 'You must
listen.' "

"Listen to what?"

"She ain't said that."

They all sat in silence.

"Jesse," Nathan said, "Roxanne thought if you was
to *know* about this, then maybe yo mother could
come through better."

"I hope so," Roxanne said. "Onlyest thing, I can't
tell *who's* gonna speak when I goes into that sleep."

"I let you know, Jesse," Nathan said.

Jesse looked back and forth between them. He
wanted so badly to learn more, tonight, not later. But
they both wanted to help him. Whatever else was
true, at least he could see that.

"All right," he finally said. "I hope you find out
something soon."

"Jesse," Nathan said, "you has got to keep this here
a secret."

"I will."

"Lemme tell you *why*. White folks round here, they
all, nearbout, go to the Baptist church."

"Yes."

"And they all believe in the life of the spirit. Yo
soul what flies on an on, on an on, long time after the

body is ashes and worms in the ground. Thas the truth?"

"That's the truth."

"All right. But now *if*, just if you tries to talk to one of them about them souls, they gonna get *mad*.

"Why is that?"

"I don't know why. Make em mad, though. They gonna tell you 'we don't kı ow nothin bout that. Thas devil's talk.' "

"My work is from Jesus," Roxanne said. "Most all of what I do is tell my friends what to eat, and what to stop eatin. I just tell em whatever them souls *says* to tell them."

"I know," Jesse said. He was beginning to feel like one of them.

"Far as folks *say*," Nathan went on, "they gone die and pass to heaven. But if you mention to em that so an so had a thing to say from over there, they gonna cast you *out!*"

"I won't say anything."

"He won't, neither," Nathan said to Roxanne.

"Pray for yo mother," Roxanne said. "I believe that what she needs the most."

Chapter 14

The next day Jesse avoided his brothers. He felt it wouldn't do any good to argue, and he was ashamed for Nathan to see him acting like one of them. So he didn't want to talk at all. But at the noon break, Robert Elmer put his long arm around Jesse's shoulders and pulled him toward the catalpa tree. He went along.

"Ain't you got somethin to tell us?" Robert Elmer asked as they came up to Bean. Jesse wanted to yell at them about attacking Nathan's house. In fact, he was thinking about giving Robert Elmer one in the stomach while he stood there, unsuspecting. But he was afraid for Nathan and Roxanne, so he held it back.

"I don't think so," he said.

"Son," Bean said smiling, "have you been thinking about our club?"

"From time to time, Bean, yeah I have."

"Good, good! That's what I like to hear."

"Your club stinks, Bean."

Robert Elmer slowly removed his arm from Jesse's shoulders.

"Aw come on—"

"No," Robert Elmer said bitterly, "let him alone, Bean. I told you he's soft."

"Yeah but—"

"But *what?*"

"Well, I just hate it so. I mean, he's our little brother and all."

"Forget him," Robert Elmer said. "Just forget him."

Jesse's stomach turned. Did he mean it? Or did he just want to make Jesse feel left out, so he'd turn around and join?

Robert Elmer stepped away from them and sat down with his lunch sack.

"Aw, Jesse," Bean said, acting embarrassed. "I didn't mean to put the heat on you. Think it over some more, okay?"

"I don't want it, Bean," he said quietly.

Bean's face flushed quickly, as if he was mad, but he settled down again. "Jesse, Paw was down to my tent last night, and he was wantin my pay from the mill."

"You give it to him?"

"Lucky for me, I'd already spent it. Every dime." He grinned. "But Paw said he was comin for yours next."

"Oh, great."

"Yeah, figured you'd like to know that. And one more thing. He's mad as he can be at Sheriff Riggins.

They had the election and he won and all, but Riggins still won't let us haul shine."

"Why not?"

"Claims he wants to let things cool down first. But Paw thinks he's lettin another guy go on ahead with his."

"Oh."

"Yeah. Paw says if it turns out to be true—"

"I know," Jesse stopped him, "I know all the things he's planning to do."

"Guess you do, little brother."

They stood there for another moment. Jesse was grateful for the warning, and for Bean not acting like Robert Elmer. Neither of them knew what to say.

Saturday morning was wet with dew, and clear. Jesse's heart was beating fast as he passed the Evans mailbox.

There was no sign of a dog, and he walked on through the carport and down around the lake to the stable.

Ren was standing beside two horses, tightening the cinch on the new one.

The Irish setter came from behind her barking, and she turned with a quick smile.

"Hush!" she cried to the dog. "Good morning! How do you like your horse?"

"Like him fine."

"He's a gelding and he's eleven years old. Name's Bad News."

He smiled.

The horse was about the same height as Raffasha. He was a bay with a white blaze on his face, and he seemed calm.

"He's over the hill as far as speed goes," she said. "But he's a good smart horse. He'll do what you tell him, as long as you know what you want."

"Whose is he?"

"He belongs to a friend of Daddy's, over in Tuscaloosa. His daughter went to college and she's not coming home this summer, so he said we could keep Bad News as long as we wanted."

"He came from over there?"

"Yep. Daddy sent a man over yesterday, with Raffasha's trailer. Just for you."

"He didn't tell me."

"He better not have! I told him it was my surprise."

"I don't know what to say, Ren."

"Well, let's see if you can ride him."

She laughed and handed him the reins.

Immediately Bad News perked up and seemed nervous.

"I'm Jesse," he said to the horse, "and you better do right."

She laughed and began showing him how to mount.

They walked around the lake until he understood his basic positions and signals.

"Let's go somewhere," she said.

"Okay."

"I better lead the way."

"Good."

They passed the carport and she dismounted and tied the dog. Then they started. At the mailbox she turned north, away from town. It was a new territory for Jesse and he was glad.

Ren trotted off down the road. He jangled up and down, smiling as she looked back laughing now and then.

After about a mile she turned sharply right on a dirt road and they headed into a stand of cottonwoods along a creek. Along it there were a few sleeping houses where even the dogs were drowsing in the early heat.

They passed a few corn and beanfields, but soon reached an unused road that wound back toward the swamp.

They rode for a few miles and Ren dismounted before a gate. It was a barbed wire and pole cattle gap, and she brought Raffasha through.

Now they took a grassy lane under low-spreading white oaks and there were no tracks ahead of them in the weeds.

They hadn't talked in a long time.

After another half mile the weeds got higher, and there were ragged little blossoms of yellow dog fennel everywhere. Queen Anne's lace and elderberry flowers floated above the Johnson grass and sage, and the smell of lush dank plants was laced here and there with sugary honeysuckle and blackberry.

"We're almost there," she said softly.

Wherever they were going, he wished the silent hot ride would never end.

They reached an untended pecan orchard. Raffasha seemed to know the way, and they angled through the old decaying trees toward a high, tin-roofed barn in the far corner.

"This was grandmother's," she said. "Daddy's mother. It was still used to store hay until last year."

They rode up to the wall, then around to the open door. Inside it was like a cathedral: tall weathered siding that admitted cracks of light, and the rich smell of hay. There was a second floor and a small third floor, and they could see the high, timbered roof.

"This is it?" Jesse whispered, following her lead.

"Yes," she whispered back, "get down."

They dismounted and she walked the horses outside, through some elderberry bushes down a slope to a shallow creek, and she let them drink a little. Then she brought them back to the barn and tethered them on long leads fastened to the barn wall.

"Does your father still own this place?"

"Yes. Almost two hundred acres of oak hollows. He says it's not much good for timber or cattle, and he guesses somebody will buy it for the hunting."

"Just for that?"

"Doctors, mostly. They have the money. This place is loaded with deer. Daddy says when the river channelization goes through it will destroy a lot of the hunting clubs, and they'll be willing to pay anything."

"Oh."

"I hope that doesn't happen."

She led the way back into the barn, and up the ladders to the third level. There were broken bales of hay everywhere.

"Are you a hunter, Jesse?"

"No. My family all are though."

They walked around the loft, looking at the heavy beams and the corrugated tin roofing, until she flopped down on a pile of hay. He sat down carefully beside her.

"Too hot for you?" she asked.

"No."

"I like to sweat."

They sat still for a long time and a pair of blue and white pigeons fluttered noisily up and landed on the flooring before them.

They gave their trilling, clucking calls as they bobbled their necks and pecked at the hay. Jesse saw a fat beetle run from its overturned hideaway, a patch of stalks, and one of the birds got it.

"Well," she said—the pigeons took off—"this is it."

"You sound kind of sad," he said.

"I don't know. I guess I wonder if I should have brought you here."

"Because you just met me?"

"Yes."

She wasn't looking at him.

"And," she said, "I'm afraid you won't think it's special enough, after such a long ride."

"Oh no. I love it."

"You do? Are you sure?"

"Yeah."

He smiled as she slowly turned to him. It was only these moments, he noticed, when she needed something from him, that he felt confident.

"Well, I hope so. I never brought but one person up here before, and that turned out horribly."

"Why?"

"A girl from school. She hated the long ride, the bugs, the hay sticking to her, the smelly horses, and, finally, no food."

They laughed.

"Good idea about the food," he said.

"I know. I brought some. But it's a surprise."

They smiled again and she lay back.

He lay down too, keeping the same distance, and he smelled the sweet dry hay.

"Ren," he finally said. "How come you're being so nice to me?"

"Well, at first I liked the idea that you grew up in the swamp, and you never went to school. I just wanted to see what you were like. But that was a little mean, I have to admit. Anyway, after I met you I liked the fact that you didn't know any of the school kids."

"Why?"

"Because I can't stand them. Daddy says I'm a snob, with my Virginia put-on ways, and I guess I am. But I don't care. I'm just biding my time to get out of here, anyway."

"That's too bad."

"Yes, it is. Mother keeps pushing me to make friends with the kids who go to our church."

"You don't want to?"

"Boring. All boring and silly."

"Didn't you grow up with these kids?"

"Yes. I liked them a lot when I was little. But since I started spending the summers with my grandparents . . ."

"I see."

"So I just go to school and do what I have to do. I spend most of my time with Raffasha."

"Are you lonesome?"

"I guess. Not for those kids, though. Mother thinks something's wrong with me, because I don't care about dancing. She thinks it's normal and healthy. I think normal and healthy is somewhere far from here. Do you understand that?"

"Yes. I think so, too." His voice became hard and brittle. "I just want to escape my family. My father, mostly."

"Every time you talk about him you get upset, don't you?"

"Yeah, probably. I used to think he just drank too much whiskey, because we had some good times when he wasn't drinking."

"But now?"

"He's mean, Ren. And the way he looks at everything . . . he thinks people are out to get him."

"Oh."

"More like, he's out to get them. He thinks your father is his enemy, by the way."

"But why?"

"He fired Paw once."

"But he's hired him again."

"I know. But Paw never forgets a grudge."

Jesse felt his stomach tighten. He looked at the huge beams in the roof and imagined hitting his father.

"And neither do I."

"Jesse?"

She was speaking softly.

"Huh?"

"Come back."

"Oh."

"Ren, I think he killed my mother. I think he pushed her, or threw her, into a flooding creek. Blue-bottom Creek."

"Jesse," she said, drawing her breath and covering her mouth with her hand.

"Yeah."

"Are you sure?"

"Robert Elmer—that's my brother—he thinks so. Nobody was there."

"Then you'll never find out."

"Maybe."

"What do you mean, maybe?"

"Ren," he said, "you might think I'm crazy, but I'm going to tell you something. Only you *can't* tell anybody, *ever*."

"All right."

"Don't say that unless you mean it."

"I promise."

"Do you know the story in the Bible where Jesus talks to spirits that have been dead a long time? Abraham and Moses?"

Jesse explained slowly about Nathan and Roxanne, and his hopes of finding out the truth from Tanya herself.

When he finished Ren didn't say anything for a long time. Then she took his hand and rose from the hay. She led him back down to the barn floor and she seemed deep in thought.

"Jesse," she said. "This could be true. I don't know, but I think it's possible. If it *is*, then your father's a very dangerous man, isn't he?"

"Yes."

"I want you to be *very* careful around him."

"I always am. But I'll tell you something else, Ren. If Roxanne finds out what I think she will, Paw better watch out for me."

She touched his arm and looked into his eyes, and from the way her face filled with sympathy Jesse figured he must look terrible.

"I've got an idea," she said.

"What?"

"Come see what I cooked."

Chapter 15

They ate fried chicken and biscuits and messy
wedges of warm lemon pie.

When they finished, Jesse asked, "Why don't I
show you my part of the woods?"

"All right."

They rode past the sawmill and up into the trees.
Jesse liked leading the way.

They passed through thick switchcane around the
beaver pond, across long hackberry flats with pale
grass in the shadows, and finally threaded their way
through some red oaks on the slope of a hill. Huge
silver beech trees stood with their roots out of the
ground, gracefully wound around boulders.

Then they came onto an old railroad path. It was
smaller than a modern one, and the rails were long
gone.

"This was in the Civil War," Jesse said.

It was just a high, grassy mound on the side of a
steep hill, with some of the old crossties still in place.

"How far?" she said softly.

"Two more miles."

They kept up the slow, steady pace, past the tangles of briar and honeysuckle, and the lush oaks and hickories.

He stopped his horse and looked back at her.

"I'm going to show you the place," he said, "where Mama died."

Bees and wasps flew by them in lazy lines.

They rode on, Jesse thinking about Tanya Watersmith, running and stumbling, maybe, along this trail. And Paw behind her.

Jesse had been there before, long ago, but he had not looked at the place the way he needed to now.

Finally they rounded a steep curve, and saw that the trail disappeared into a dark tunnel in the hill.

"We go in there?" Ren asked, smiling at him.

"Yes," he said.

"You've been through before?"

"Yes. There's a little curve. It's okay."

She reached forward and patted Raffasha.

"You heard him," she said. "Our friend Jesse says this tunnel is safe."

Raffasha seemed indifferent.

They entered the darkness.

The air inside was much cooler, and smelled of wet clay and moss. Underground springs dripped with loud echoes on the stones, and cold little sprays bounced on their skin.

"Helloooo," Ren said, listening to her voice ring. And the horses' hooves clacked in the rock darkness like electrified drums.

They came to the curve in the tunnel and barely saw the light before hitting the wall.

They had another fifty yards to go.

Just ahead an animal jumped and ran for the opening.

"Go faster!" Jesse said.

Ren hugged Raffasha with her legs and the mare lept ahead.

The hooves rang on the stones and they were within twenty-five yards of the circle of daylight when the bobcat burst through, first a silhouetted black ball against the brightness and then, in the moment of escape, the long, stretched-out, brown-furred form.

Bad News and Raffasha burst from the darkness and the bobcat was gone.

They stopped and stood looking far down the steep slope into the brush and trees.

"Did you get a good look?" Jesse whispered.

"Yes," Ren said, "she was flying."

"Look," he said.

Up ahead about a hundred yards stood the old railroad bridge. Most of it had been burned a long time ago, and only the tressel structure was left, with a single wide beam spanning the deep creek.

Midway across the beam was the bobcat. It was still, looking back over its shoulder. Then it turned and walked slowly on its graceful way, twitching its tail.

Jesse dismounted, tied his reins to a sapling, and walked ahead.

It had not rained in a long time, and as he approached the bridge, he saw dry, gravelly sides dropping down into the creekbed. Then he was close, and saw that the water was only a foot deep, and it was sparkling clear.

The one long beam over the banks was charred on the edges, as were most of the timbers in the tressel. But it still seemed solid, and he took the first step. He looked over his shoulder and saw Ren, sitting on Raffasha, holding back and watching.

He took another step.

So a bobcat stays around here, he thought.

What was it like in the flood?

Was the water high, nearly over the tressel beams?

And was she tired when she got this far?

He looked back over his shoulder at Ren. Tanya must have turned like this and seen Twaint, coming to get her. No telling what he said, what he yelled at her.

Did he catch her?

Jesse walked on, balancing with his arms held wide.

He reached the center of the creek. Was this it? The last step for my mother? He looked at the billowy trees, lush with summer leaves. The grasshoppers and cicadas sang low. It was a magic spot. He felt that. No wonder a bobcat was here.

He turned and walked lightly back to the bank.

Ren brought the mare up to him and dismounted.

She took his hand.

"This is where my mother died," he said.

"I'm sorry," she whispered.

She put her arms around him and they hugged each other.

"Do you think he killed her?" he finally said.

She looked into his eyes and felt his confusion and pain.

"I don't know. Nobody knows that," she whispered.

"Except him, damn him."

"Don't say that."

"Why not?"

"It will make you sick. It won't help."

"I'm going to get him," Jesse said. "He killed her, and now he's killing Aunt May."

"You don't know that."

Jesse looked at the deep crevice of the creekbed. Ren's arms were still lightly around him. He turned back to her and said, "You're right. I don't know. But if he did, if he really did kill her, then I'm going to kill *him*."

"Don't say that," she whispered, touching his lips.

"No, listen," he said. "I'll have to fight him anyway if Aunt May and I are going to get away. I've been forgetting all about it. Acting like there wasn't any problem."

"No," she said, "no."

"But there is, Ren. I don't want to fight him. I don't even know whether I *can* fight him. But I do know this. If he killed my mother, I can kill him. I can do it, and I will."

"Hush," she whispered. "You'll never really know about that."

"Yes I will," he said. "I will know."

He looked into her eyes.

Jesse felt a strange, sudden calmness just because he had decided exactly what he was going to do.

"My mother," he said. "My mother is going to tell me the truth."

Chapter 16

That night as Jesse approached Miss Elmilly's house he heard a crash inside.

The lights were out even though it had been full dark for half an hour.

He ran up the steps, across the porch, and opened the door. There was a muffled cry from the kitchen.

He took long strides across the creaking floor and stopped in the kitchen doorway.

Miss Elmilly's feet were sticking out in the darkness toward his stomach. Then he heard Paw's low chuckling in his throat. Jesse reached out and silently switched on the overhead light. Paw was standing there, squinting in the harsh light and grinning. He had Miss Elmilly stretched out on the table, a rag stuffed into her mouth, and his big arm around her skinny throat. Her eyes were glazed over in the glare.

"What are you doing?!" Jesse screamed.

"Don't get upset," Paw said with a whiskey slur. "I didn't come to see her anyway."

He let go of her and she tried to roll over but seemed paralyzed.

Jesse reached out and took her hands in his, and slowly pulled her upright, keeping his eyes level on Paw's.

Then he took hold of the rag in her mouth, a rough cotton kitchen towel with faded yellow stripes, and gently tugged on it, as if he were trying to coax it from a dog. Slowly, Miss Elmilly Robertson opened her mouth and let it go.

"I come to see *you*," Paw said, as cheerfully as if nothing had happened.

Jesse was shaking. He wanted to tear Paw to pieces. He took Miss Elmilly's stick-thin arms and slid her toward him across the formica table. She was still in a sitting position, and she landed bent over. He held her and pulled her upright. Then he stepped aside, as if teaching her to walk alone through the door. She managed to do it.

"Now," Jesse said, "now you are gonna see me."

"Spunky as a rooster," Paw said. "But *listen*—" he dropped his smile and pointed a knobby finger at Jesse— "I come here to collect your pay. That woman claimed you don't keep it here."

"You want something from me, you ask me for it."

"Where's your damn money?"

"Paw, don't you see what you've done?"

"What? What's your old bad Paw done?" He smiled, easily, again.

"Drop the 'poor old Paw' act. You had no call to lay a hand on Miss El . . ."

"Shut up, boy! Just shut up!"

He grabbed a straight-backed cane chair and lifted it high, smashed it hard against the refrigerator.

The humming of the old, round-shouldered machine grew louder for an instant, then stopped, leaving an aftersound like a final gasp.

"That's great, Paw. Just great. Break things, destroy things. That's all you know, isn't it?"

"I'll break you, boy, you don't give me the money."

"You need money, Paw?" Jesse dropped his arms and his fists uncoiled, and against his will tears started down his face. "You need some money? I'll give you some money. Why couldn't you ask me for it?"

"Don't cry, you little baby," Paw said.

Jesse realized by the way Paw said it that he was very drunk. Paw leaned heavily against the table. "Give me the money, now," he said, "and I'll go way and leave you lone."

Jesse stood staring at him. He looked raw and gray in the overhead glare. His eye-bags were heavy, and his pupils were full of red lightning.

"That's what you want, ain't it? Want me to go way and stop bothering you. I know. You don't want your old Paw no more."

"It's not that simple."

"Huh? Sure it is. You don't come see me up there. You ain't asked nobody about me."

Jesse couldn't believe Paw cared.

"You turnin into a town boy, ain't you? Never comin back to the woods again, are you?"

"I never said that."

"Shut up. Give me your money."

"Wait for me out on the porch, Paw," he said levelly.

"Oh, sure."

"I mean it. Get out there and wait a minute. I'll bring it to you."

Paw walked past him, stopping for an instant and leaning over into Jesse's face and staring into his eyes. He searched there as if he were looking for something he had lost, and then he grinned and went on out to the front porch.

Jesse walked into Miss Elmilly's bedroom but she was gone. He went out the back door of the house and she was sitting on the sandstone ledge by the fence.

"Are you all right?" he whispered.

"Yes, I think so," she rasped, her long fingers on her veiny neck.

"Paw's on the porch. I'll get rid of him in a minute."

"Don't," she said, grabbing his arm. "Stay here, or run."

"No," he said, "you just wait."

He walked back inside and went to his bedroom. He took down the old framed picture on the wall, an image of Miss Elmilly young with a parasol and a ruffly dress and a smile. Behind it, in the crack of the cardboard backing, he felt the edges of his bills. He pulled them all out, rolled them up, and stuffed them into his pocket. He was furious with himself for paying attention to Paw's plea for sympathy. Then he took the bottle of flowers from the bureau. It was an old fashioned milk bottle of thick glass, and he pulled out the daisies Miss Elmilly had picked and dropped them on the floor. He poured the water out the open window. Then he dried off the neck with his bed-sheet, and clenched his teeth. He walked to the living room and across the floor to the front door. He stopped there for a moment, drawing a deep breath. Finally he held the bottle out of sight behind his leg and stepped onto the porch.

He still had not decided whether to give his father the money or crash the bottle over his head when he realized the man was gone.

Sunday morning Jesse woke up thinking of ways to kill his father. He remembered his dreams, struggles with Bean and Robert Elmer, wrestling and fighting them in the mud, always with Twaint standing there, smiling, looking on.

Miss Elmilly called him to breakfast.

He thought about killing Paw all the way through his eggs and sausage and biscuits.

They didn't talk much during breakfast. But Jesse felt the night before had created a sad bond between them. As soon as he could excuse himself, Jesse headed toward the swamp.

Each step was full of his new purpose. When he reached the dense woods, a stand of water oaks straight and dark and tall, he stood there as if he were one of them. He seemed to be drawing strength from them.

Then he walked on into the swamp, until he came

to the beaver dam. He eased up to it, his arms sliding
and hissing on the stalks and sharp leaves of cane.
When he could see the water he stood perfectly still
and waited.

The surface was a pool of glass. A bumblebee
sailed past his ear, the only thing stirring in the
muggy heat. Along the far bank, just in the water,
there was movement. A beaver started swimming beside the bank, its nose and head cutting a neat wake
in the surface. Suddenly the rough log above it on
the bank moved. It was an alligator! It was going
now, and as the beaver stopped, turned, and began
to submerge, the alligator shot off its lazy perch and
thrashed the water with the struggling fat beaver in
its jaws. With a last violent flick of its tail the gator
disappeared beneath the surface.

Jesse watched the ripples settle, until the pool was
a bright, black mirror again.

He walked on around the pond, watching for
snakes, and listening to the hundreds of turtles plop
into the water as they heard his footsteps.

Then he headed up toward camp, and slipped into
the trees on its edge. He saw his father, shirtless,
stretched out on the grass in front of his trailer, and
Aunt May was on her knees over him, rubbing his
back.

How can she touch him? Jesse thought. Is he making her do it? She rubbed a long while, then suddenly
got up and walked into the trailer. Jesse crouched in
the shadows and waited. She came back down carrying a fruit jar of moonshine, and Jesse wasn't sure

but he thought she was smiling. Paw sat beside her on the steps. When Jesse saw them sharing the open jar his stomach turned a flip, and he melted backwards into the woods.

He was dripping with sweat. He felt as though he were swimming in the thick air. He started east toward the railroad bridge, confused and grateful that he was alone. He walked a long time, his feelings rushing and his mind blank, and finally came to the mounded grassy track of the old railroad, and then within sight of the cave. He remembered now the story Aunt May had told him long before, about the last train to make this run. It was a Confederate supply train toward the end of the war, and except for the engineer the entire crew was young boys, not a one over sixteen. They were rushing medical supplies to the hospitals in the east, and they were going much faster than usual because there hadn't been troop movements here for months, and the Yankees weren't supposed to care about stopping this particular train.

So they skipped checking the bridge, and when they came out of the tunnel and got halfway over the chasm it blew clear up past the treetops. That was how Aunt May put it.

It killed every one of those boys. Aunt May still remembered pieces of iron lying about in the creekbed, when she was a girl. But they had all been carried off or buried by floods. And the bridge had been rebuilt, but later it burned.

Jesse entered the cool dark tunnel. He listened to

his feet on the stones, and the echo each step made. Bats came unstuck from the walls and fluttered frantically up and down past him. He walked faster.

When he came to the curve he started to run. Around he went, toward the circle of yellow bright daylight. The last ride for those boys, he was thinking. Faster and faster he came on, his feet ringing, the bats shooting off, and he listened to the chugging of that old steam train, carrying those angry boys on their last ride.

He ran out into the light and kept running toward the bridge. Their last fifty yards, he thought, just like my mother's. He spread his arms straight out for balance and kept his stride as he hit the long timber across the gulf.

It would be an easy run if it were on the ground, he thought. He was looking straight ahead, trying not to think about the drop, and he got the feel of it enough to speed up.

Then he saw the rattlesnake. It was stretched out long on the beam with its head toward him. He reached the center of the bridge and it was only a few feet ahead. As he tried to slow himself the snake raised up a little, then higher and higher; it was trying to coil and weaving violently from side to side. Jesse knew he couldn't stop. He stretched his long legs out for the last few steps and jumped as high as he could. He was in the air when he saw the snake coming up, straight out of its coil at him, and he felt something bang his foot. Now he was falling and his head and arms were too far out in front of his legs. He spread his arms and hit the beam on his chest, sliding as his shirt tore and the skin burned. He was kicking his feet hard behind him and slapping his arms and palms on the sides of the beam, trying to have a grip ready when his sliding stopped.

Then he stopped, hugging the beam tightly and smashing his feet up and down behind him. He drew himself up into a ball and looked back. There was no snake. He was shaking too hard to examine his feet, afraid he'd fall off. He pressed his face into the wood and rested a long time. Finally he crawled over to the far bank.

It was then he saw the rattlesnake again.

It had fallen off the timber, and was down in the creekbed writhing in steady rhythmic curves, back and forth but without going anywhere.

Jesse stood, unsteady, and walked to a spot where he thought he could climb down. But it was too steep. He sat down and slid, first by the seat of his pants and then on his back, too, and he landed in the clear shallow water in a rumble of gravel and dust.

The snake was a few feet away, trapped by something. Jesse looked around for a weapon. Then he felt a jab in his back. He rolled over and touched a sharp piece of metal covered with layers and layers of flake rust. He pulled and it gave a little. He stood up and gripped it with both hands and jerked, and out come the iron bar.

The rattler had landed on a rock. Its skin was not broken, and Jesse couldn't tell what was wrong with it, but it just kept up the crazy curves in place, unable somehow to move.

It took him ten blows to kill it.

It was seven feet long and had fifteen rattles. He pulled his knife from his pocket and cut them off, then carefully put them in his shirt pocket.

His arms and chest burned, and he was full of splinters. He took off his clothes and shoes and examined his feet, but there was no sign of a bite. It must have hit his shoe. He washed himself and then lay on his back, letting the water gurgle around him.

He looked up at the puffy white clouds scuddling in the blue sky. A breeze came up, and the lush trees swished loudly.

But Jesse's teeth were clenched.

His mind was on those boys, his age, riding the rebel train through the rock cave for the last time. His fists were tight. He relived that last turn inside the rock, their hatred of the Yankees. By that time in the war the south was about bled out, and the remaining armies were being replenished by old men and young boys. They felt a frustration and hopeless determination to go on and die just because every single soul they knew and respected had already done it . . .

So they came around the bend and hit the dynamite bridge over the creek. What season? If it was summer, and the creek was low, they had a long fall—from the top of their arc—down into this murmuring clear water. And if it was flood time, then the fire hardly had time to flash out the train windows before all was extinguished in a brief loud explosion of steam.

He rose up on his elbows, shaking with anger. He

imagined those boys from the train, standing all around him right this minute, just as sorrowful and angry as ever.

He got up and put on his clothes, and found a place to climb back up to the railroad bed.

He crossed the beam again, without flinching or looking down.

Then he took one last long look around, filled with a strange furious power from the place.

All the way back to town he was thinking of what to say to Nathan and Roxanne, to get them to hurry.

Chapter 17

The sawblade whined furiously as it bit into a red oak log. Fresh pink boards were floating down the chain to Robert Elmer and Bean, and Jesse beside them.

"You missed a good one Saturday night," Bean hollered.

"Yeah?"

"Oh Lordy. Robert Elmer and Gloria got up and danced on the bartop. They must have stomped thirty glasses."

Jesse didn't smile.

"And *me*," Bean laughed as he yelled over the saw noise, "I had two women dancin with me, out in the middle of the floor. And their husbands was sittin at each end of the bar, drinkin whiskey and rubbin their fists."

"How'd you get out?" Jesse yelled.

"Both them sapsuckers came for me at the same time! I left them women where I found em and lit out the door."

"Was anybody after Robert Elmer?"

"Huh?"

"Robert Elmer. Anybody after him?"

"Oh. Naw. Her husband's out of the hospital though. He'll be around soon."

Jesse looked over at Robert Elmer. He didn't seem scared. Just the same old hungover-grayface he always was.

They pulled the boards without talking for a long time, and a little past midmorning the big mill engine broke down. All the men sat wherever they could find shade and smoked. Jesse, with his brothers, walked over to the catalpa tree.

He caught a quick glimpse of Nathan, who looked strangely at him, then quickly shook his head and walked away.

Jesse pulled the rough oak boards all afternoon, and every one hit his hands as a piece of Twaint Watersmith. When he tossed them into their racks, he was tossing Paw, and when a reject had to be pitched far across the bunks to a pile, that was Paw going down into the railroad creek.

That night Miss Elmilly asked him about his lessons, but he wasn't interested. He told her he had some things on his mind, and he would spend the next week or so reading and working problems on his own.

Then, as soon as he could politely excuse himself after supper, he went walking toward the black part of town.

Nathan was sitting on his porch with his fox.

"Hello," Jesse said.

"Thas you all right," Nathan said from his rocker. "Thas what she said. She said, 'Tonight is when he comin, you wait.' "

"Huh?" Jesse opened the gate and came into the yard.

"She gone to bed, young man."

"What?" Jesse said, walking up the steps.

"Sit down," Nathan said. "You see that rockin chair?"

"Yes."

"I sittin here savin it for you."

"You were? How'd you—"

"Because Missy Roxanne said to me, 'Tonight he comin. He full of trouble. You watch!' "

"Did she talk with my . . . I mean, did—"

"Sit down," Nathan said. "Rest yo feet."

Jesse sat down in the rocker. The fox sniffed his legs.

"You haven't heard anything from my mother?"

"No. She asked, whenever she say her prayers. And then she got *me* to ask, when she go off into her sleep. But we ain't heard nothing yet."

"I see," Jesse said.

"What's botherin you, boy?"

"Can I talk to Roxanne?"

"It's a funny thing," Nathan said. "I shouldn't tell you none of this, but she didn't want to see you tonight. She know you was comin, and it upset her. She was holdin her stomach and walkin around the house, sayin, 'He carryin too much. He carryin more than he can carry.' "

"Can't I—"

"She gone to bed. It upset her stomach and she went right to bed."

"I'm sorry," Jesse said.

"Young man, they's a plenty young men in this neighborhood, right here, that had good folks and they *still* dropped off. They was raised *right*, and they gone right straight to the gutter. You understand me?"

"I guess so."

"And then, they's plenty more that had folks you couldn't pay me to have. Drunks, whores, they's the good and the bad down here. And some them young men I'm tellin you about come from them families."

"Yes?"

"My own son, Charlie."

There was a long pause.

"He ain't worth a nickel."

The fox had put her head up in Jesse's lap.

"What I'm tryin to tell you," Nathan said, "is they's a many a burden to be carried in this world. And you jus *can't* let the devil tell you to lie down and quit. He always up *to* that. That his *business*."

"The devil."

"Thas right. He try to get you to feel so sorry fo yo self that you quit."

"I see."

"And when you quit, then you drinks whiskey and carries on, leavin a trail of babies behind you—do you understand me?"

"I reckon."

"You bein tempted right now. Roxanne, she can feel this. And I *believe* her."

"Nathan, there's something I want to ask my mother."

They sat there in the dark without saying anything.

"And, I wanted to ask Roxanne if she could do that."

"Sometimes," Nathan said. "What you want to know?"

"Well, I was thinking, maybe I wouldn't have to *say* it. I mean, if Roxanne *knows* things like she does, then she could just *tell*."

"I see."

"I mean, maybe my mother will know, and she can just give Roxanne the answer."

"She don't give Roxanne the answers, she *take over* Roxanne and give them to *me*."

"That's what I meant."

"Well, I don't know, boy. I reckon it won't hurt to try."

Chapter 18

The next afternoon as Jesse walked from the mill he heard hoofbeats coming behind him.

Ren was smiling and he was, too, as he stood there wiping the sawdust and sweat from his face.

"Want to take a ride after supper?"

"Sure."

"Shall I come for you with the horses?"

"Please do."

"Know what?"

"Huh?"

"We've *got* to get you saddling your own mount!"

They laughed together and she galloped off.

Ren coming to Miss Elmilly's for him! He hadn't wanted to think of it because he wondered if she would—if her mother would let her.

He walked home thinking how Ren lightened his thoughts so easily.

He was humming softly and Miss Elmilly yelled through the door to inquire about his good mood.

"Going riding with Ren after supper," he said. "What are we having?"

"Vegetable soup! And you better wash out that hair!"

"Yes, ma'am."

"What about your lessons?"

"Uh, I'll catch up."

"That's what I thought!"

Jesse smiled and lathered up his face. But something was eating at him. He had expected Aunt May to move to town long before now. It was suddenly clear to him that she was avoiding it. He *had* to get her out of that camp before he moved against Paw.

Ren came a little late, under the clear sky filling with rose and lavender bands and the chimney swifts flashing their shadowy forms on the chase for mosquitoes.

They rode the horses up toward the mill, then past it and into the trees. They came within a hundred yards of the brothers' tents but they weren't in sight.

"Ren," he said, "I need to talk with my aunt. Do you think we could head up there now?"

"How far is it?"

"About four miles. It's past that beaver dam I showed you."

"Well, if you don't mind riding fast."

"Your folks won't worry?"

"I could call them from the mill."

"Good."

She rode back down and made the call. He watched her from a distance, waving her arm for emphasis as she argued. Finally she came back.

"I've got to make it home by eleven."

"Let's go then."

"Jesse."

"Yes."

"He wouldn't try anything with me there, would he?"

"I don't think so."

"All right."

They rode as fast as they could in the falling darkness. High stars spread across the purple sky above the trees, and a little wind came up.

Jesse was sure he knew the way well enough but he was grateful when the waning full moon rose and caught in the high branches ahead. When they reached the cane thickets by the beaver pond they were sweating, and he stopped a minute to let the breeze cool them. Then the moon inched higher and they could see each other clearly.

An owl cackled close by in the hackberry trees.

Jesse smiled at Ren. Her home and family were like nothing he had known—the things they talked about, sweeping in the whole world it seemed in their concerns, dazzled Jesse and gave him a calmness: worrying over others was a way of not worrying too much about yourself. Ren had such an elegant way of tossing her head, her long hair floating back, and laughing. It seemed to make light of anything mean and low and bitter. When he was with her, all his hatred seemed to fade, and the idea of killing anybody appeared too silly for words. Still, he thought, I'm a Watersmith. I'll never be a part of her world.

They almost reached camp and he told her to wait.

He slipped up to the edge and looked through the bushes. Aunt May was hobbling past her stove. She was bent nearly to the waist, leaning on a long stick.

"Aunt May!" he said, running to her.

They hugged, and she told him that Paw hadn't come in that night at all. Then he brought Ren and the mare to camp.

The moon was bright in the clearing.

"So *you* the one Miss Elmilly's tellin about! You pretty enough!"

Aunt May's soft, leathery face lit up with wrinkles when she smiled.

"Why are you so bent over?" Jesse asked.

"That old man come in drunk the other night," she said, waving her stick, "and he shoved me down."

"No!" Ren said.

"I twisted somethin in my back. I reckon I'll get over it."

"That's horrible!" Ren said. "Why don't you leave here?"

"Sounds to me like he been tellin you things," Aunt May said, scowling at Jesse.

"I'm sorry," Ren said, "I didn't mean to butt in."

"That's all right," Aunt May said. "Elmilly told me you was a smart thing."

"She's right, Aunt May," he said. "I came to ask you to leave here, with me."

"Leave here?" She looked back and forth at them.

"Will you?"

"I . . . well, where would I go?"

"For a start, you know you could come to Miss Elmilly's with me."

"Ain't enough room," she said.

"You can have my bedroom. I'll sleep on a cot in the front room."

"And what we gonna do when Twaint comes lookin for us?"

"I don't know about that yet."

"I think you might have to go a lot farther away, Jesse. He's already rantin and ravin about you."

"Why not have him arrested?" Ren asked.

They both looked at her with irritation.

"I'm just trying to help," she said. "He ought to be locked up, from all I've heard."

"He ought to," Aunt May said. "Just ain't no man to do it, that's all."

Aunt May took a step and fell heavily against her stick, then eased down onto the ground.

"What is it?" Jesse cried.

"My back," she said, her face contorted in pain.

"What should we do?" Ren asked.

"I don't know," she said, "it's killing me."

She twisted from side to side on the hard-packed earth and found a less painful position.

"Right there," she said, "it ain't so bad right there."

"Has this ever happened before?" Jesse asked.

"One time. I lay down for a half a day."

"What happened then?" Ren asked.

"Old snake came into camp. Big brown moccasin. I jumped up like a young girl and got my stick."

They all laughed.

She tried to move and winced again.

"Is there anything we can get you?" Ren asked.

"Yes . . ." she hesitated. "Yes, there is. Go over

yonder to the trailer and bring me a fruit jar of moonshine."

"Okay," he said and started over.

"Wait!" she cried. "Don't touch the brand new batch. All shiny new jars stacked together. Some of it's got that shaving lotion. Get me an old one from the bottom shelf."

It hurt her to raise up enough to swallow, but she managed to drink an inch down in the jar.

"Didn't know I was a drinkin gal?" She smiled at Jesse.

He knew. He had seen her with Paw. "I think we need to get you to town," he said.

"Not right now," she said, smiling and twisting her face with pain at the same time. She motioned for Ren to lift the jar to her lips again. "Right now I couldn't move if a snake was on top of me."

She closed her eyes and looked more peaceful.

"Renly," she said slowly, "Elmilly told me about you, long time ago."

"She used to give me chocolate milk every morning. And cookies and Bible stories."

"Bible stories! Now that's somethin old Jesse here is short on."

"Not as short as you think," he said.

She opened her eyes on that. "Oh? Renly, give me another pull on the whiskey jar."

"Yes, ma'am."

"You feel better?" Jesse asked.

"Got to celebrate," she said, sitting up for a swallow.

"What?"

"You," she said, laughing. "You and Renly bein friends."

She lay back and closed her eyes again.

"Y'all fine," she said. "I do believe yo mama was right."

They waited.

"She told me over and over, he's different. I just know he is. But, Jesse, she wasn't sure."

Aunt May's voice drifted a little.

"She gave up on the others. Didn't even talk to them no more. And she made me promise . . ."

"What, Aunt May?"

"Oh . . . well, that I wouldn't tell you why she . . . I mean, until you were old enough . . ."

"Aunt May?" he said, alarmed. "What did you promise?"

"Give me another swallow, honey."

Ren lifted the jar to her lips. Jesse watched drops of the clear liquid run down her wrinkled chin.

When her head was settled on the ground again and her eyes were closed, Jesse said, "What did you promise?"

The old woman's eyes snapped open.

"She . . ."

There was not a breath. The wind was dead still.

"Why she left, the day she fell off that bridge," Aunt May said, closing her eyes again. "The railroad bridge."

"She fell off?"

"Down into the floodwater," Aunt May said.

"She *fell?*" he asked. "How could she fall?"

"I promised to wait . . . till now, I reckon. If this ain't the time, I don't know when it will be. She was runnin away from here, away from him."

"And leaving me? And you?"

"Yes. She wanted me to wait to tell you, till you was old enough that you would understand."

"That she had to run off and leave her child?"

"She was a fragile thing, Jesse. I was always takin care of her. And Robert Elmer and Bean wore her out. She stayed on and on, year after year, thinkin to get them raised. And they went just like Twaint. Where's that jar?"

"Here," Ren said.

"And she didn't think I was worth it? She figured I was just like them?"

"Honey," Aunt May said with her eyes on him, "you was four years old. You loved the trapline and your older brothers more than anything. You was covered with mud day and night. And she was givin up, losin her strength."

Jesse didn't say anything. Aunt May closed her eyes.

"After you think about it, maybe you can fault her. I can't, and I'm the one who's done her work these last years."

"Did he beat her?"

"The last year was when he started. He never touched me in those days, just her. Now—"

"I know," Jesse said.

"Yes, son," she said. "You are right about us leaving here."

"Tonight," he said, "right now. You're not gonna spend another—"

"No," she said. "I can't move tonight."

"When?" Ren asked.

"The first day I can," she said. "The first time I feel strong enough to walk to town."

"I can't just leave you like this," Jesse said.

"You got to, boy. I'll be all right. My back's a little better now."

She took the whiskey jar herself and raised it.

"Moonshine," she smiled in a gentle croaking voice, "has its purposes."

"How did she fall off the bridge?" Jesse asked.

"He was chasin her. He was half crocked and runnin after her through the swamp."

"Did he . . . did he push her in?"

"No. She was just runnin over that little beam and she slipped."

"How do you know?"

"Hush, now, boy. Let me rest."

"We can't leave her here," Ren said.

"Got to," she said. "No choice. I can't move today. Let me be. I lived a long time up here, didn't I?"

"Yes."

"Well then."

"Promise me you'll come in on Saturday," Jesse said.

"Saturday. That ought to be all right."

"No later than Saturday night, hear?"

"Yes, sir! That'll just give me time to get over this girl's whiskey."

"*My* whiskey!"

"Go on now. Hurry, before I ask for another medicine bottle."

They mounted the horses and left Aunt May lying on the ground.

Then they rode through the woods under the waning moon without talking.

When they reached the sawmill field, Ren pulled her small watch out of her pocket and said it was just ten.

"Good. We made it."

"Yes."

"Thanks for going with me," he said.

"That's all right."

"I went to see Nathan last night."

"Did he know anything?"

"No. But I asked him whether I could speak to Tanya myself, through Roxanne."

"What did he say?"

"He said we could try. He didn't know."

"They call that a seance, Jesse."

"They do?"

"Yes. Lots of people believe in it. When are you going to try it?"

"I don't know. But I'm going to ask Nathan if we can try it Saturday night."

"I want to come."

"You do? I don't know—that means . . ."

"Telling Nathan and Roxanne that I know."

"Yeah."

"Can you do that?"

"Let me think about it."

"All right. But I want to be there."

"I'll try to talk to him tomorrow night."

"Jesse."

"Yes."

"No matter what you find out, no matter what Roxanne says in her trance . . ."

"Yes?"

"Don't kill your father. I know it's the wrong thing to do."

Chapter 19

The next evening, Jesse told Nathan and Roxanne that Ren knew. Roxanne rose heavily from her kitchen chair and disappeared into the bedroom. Jesse felt miserable, as if he had betrayed a trust, and Nathan sat without speaking to him for a long time.

Then Roxanne came back in, her eyes puffy and her cheeks glistening, and said she could understand it, and she knew the Evans girl could be trusted, and they should come quietly at ten o'clock Saturday night. They should each bring a Bible to hold.

Jesse thanked them and ran all the way home in his excitement. He lay in his bed late into the night, wide awake, his heart beating fast. He tried to ignore a voice somewhere inside that kept asking: But what are you going to do if you learn nothing at all?

Saturday was a hot day, and Ren and Jesse gave Raffasha and Bad News baths at the stable. They rubbed lather all over them, then rinsed them down with a hose and stroked the water away with a sweat scraper. The horses loved it. Ren had to attend a family supper, so Jesse left early and walked back to Miss Elmilly's. He was to meet Ren at the mailbox at nine. All the way home he kept hearing her laughter, and seeing her brown long arms working on Raffasha.

He expected Aunt May to be at Miss Elmilly's, but she wasn't. She still hadn't shown up when he finished supper. He walked out onto the front porch. The light was slowly fading from a few peach colored clouds, and stars were beginning to show. He sat down in the rocker, smiling to himself and savoring his memories of the afternoon. Surely Aunt May would arrive soon.

Now he felt he might actually become a part of Ren's world after all. She cared for him more than any friend he'd ever had. There was a strangeness he saw in the way he was pushing his revenge against his father to the finish, and yet becoming involved with the peacefulness of Ren at the same time. It split him in two, but there was something about the desperation, the hopeless frailty, of the situation that he liked. That must be another thing I've got inside me from Paw, he thought, because he seems to love anything extreme and reckless.

He was about to get up and head to Ren's house when he heard the rotten muffler of his brothers' old pickup.

He looked up the street and they were driving fast, skidding to a stop in front, waving a whiskey jar and yelling at him from inside the cab. Miss Elmilly appeared behind him on the porch.

Bean jumped out and swung over the gate.

"Let's go, Jesse! Let's go, boy!"

"Go where?"

"Good place!"

"I bet it is. Like the last one you took me?"

"Come *on*, boy. Ain't got time to argue!"

Bean grinned and started mashing Miss Elmilly's marigolds beside the walk.

"Hey!" Jesse yelled, jumping off the porch.

"Jesse!" Robert Elmer cried. He was standing beside the truck now.

"What?"

"You go with us, or we stomp every flower in this yard."

"That's right!" Bean laughed, crushing another marigold.

"All right!" Jesse said. "I'll settle this away from here."

He started for the truck and Miss Elmilly yelled, "You don't have to go anywhere with them!"

"That's all right," he said to her, getting in, "I'll be back."

They were well into the whiskey jar, and Robert Elmer drove fast down the hill road to the highway. He turned east and ran it up to seventy. Bean was singing snatches of a country song about an all-night fight.

Jesse was by the window, his arm out, catching the rushing wind of the night that was finally cooling off. He decided just to wait for a chance to escape. June bugs and giant moths spiraled into the headlights and popped against the windshield. Bean kept drinking and trying to sing, having his own private party.

"What are you so happy over?" Jesse asked him.

"Why, it's Saturday night, boy! Ain't that enough?"

Jesse didn't answer.

"I reckon so, too," Robert Elmer said in his dead-pan voice.

"Listen at him," Bean said. "You'd never think it to hear the way he talks atcha, but he's gonna get it from the silver queen of The Water Hole scene! Eeee-haaaaah!"

"What the hell is that?" Jesse asked, though he remembered Nathan's description of the place.

"Well, now, The Water Hole is this joint down on the highway. There's a mess of places on the strip, but The Water Hole is the one that's crawlin with them divorcees."

"Oh, I see."

"He sees, Robert El! He sees!" Bean elbowed his older brother and laughed hard.

"Maybe he does," Robert Elmer said dully.

"Well, anyway," Bean went on, "there's a couple of *young* ones, and we been tellin em all about you."

"Oh?"

"Oh *yeah*," Bean said, "tonight could be your night!"

Jesse looked up at the clear stars.

During the hours with Ren he had lost his hatred and, with it, his confidence in handling his brothers and Paw.

She had made him remember all the gentleness of their time together, and he had been sitting on the porch thinking of it.

His brothers had broken into his thoughts like a stone on the still surface of the pond.

They slowed up and passed a row of small block buildings with their front doors hanging open and colored lights flickering from inside. Some had portable electric signs in front, with huge arrows of white bulbs flashing off and on, pointing the way in.

"This must be it," Jesse said.

"The strip," Bean said. "Every man out here carries at least a knife."

The last place on the strip was the largest, and Robert Elmer pulled roughly off the highway there.

The Water Hole, read its sign, with the final two letters missing.

"All out!" Bean said. "This where the action is *at!*"

As he walked toward the front door Bean put his arm around Jesse's shoulders and said, in a soft serious voice, "Just stick close to us and watch your back."

They walked inside and the oval bar was nearly full of people. Some of them waved through the haze of the cigarette smoke and spoke to the brothers, a few turned their heads the other way.

They found three barstools in a row and sat down.

"Don't try to bring that wildcat whiskey in here," the bartender said. She was a big meaty woman with tattoos.

"What cat?" Bean grinned.

"Don't fool with me," she said. "My boss may buy it from you and make me sell it over the counter, but any that touches your ugly lips in here will be bought and paid for."

"Nasty nasty." Bean winked at Jesse.

"Gimme a glass of Jim Beam," Robert Elmer said.

"Yeah, me too," Bean said. "High class tonight."

"How old is thisun?"

"He's twenty-one last Sunday," Bean said. "Do you think he looks like us?"

"If he's twenty-one I'm the queen of Alabama," the woman said. "And as for lookin like you two, I'll give him the benefit and say no."

"I'll ignore that remark," Bean said cheerfully, "if you'll serve me up a glass of beer for a chaser."

"If the law comes in here—"

"Woman," Robert Elmer said, "you and the rest of the county knows you got the law so paid off he don't know where this place is."

She slid the drinks across the bar and moved away from them.

"Jesse," Bean said, "we need to talk to you. Our papa is back in the whiskey business."

"He's still working for Mr. Evans."

"He was the other night when we seen him. But he's mad as hell. You know Evans bought the timber off the sheriff's mother's old place, and Paw's been working up there with the crew."

"Yeah."

"Well, Paw, he says he *knows* the sheriff's done double-crossed him bad, lettin somebody else haul shine. He's plannin somethin for Riggins, I ain't sure what. And he's got that big bunch of whiskey needin deliverin."

The lady barkeep happened by and heard that. "Why don't the skunk let it age a little?"

"Go do it with a frog," Bean said. "One of these old days," he said to Jesse, "she's gonna get hers."

Jesse heard welcoming voices near the door and he looked around to see a woman coming toward them. She was young and very shapely, with an exaggerated sashaying walk. Her face was finely made, held aloof and stern, and her hair was a perfect silver creation of the beauty shop.

Robert Elmer jumped off his barstool and smiled at her.

"Here she comes," Bean said to Jesse.

She walked up to them, parting the waves of blue cigarette smoke that hung suspended in the air.

"Gloria," Bean said, "this is our little brother, Jesse."

"I need a drink," Gloria said.

Robert Elmer pushed a small man off the next seat and took it, giving Gloria his place beside Bean.

"Jesse," Bean went on cheerfully, "this here's Gloria Perkins."

"Pleased to meetcha," Gloria said, slamming her small fist down on the bar. "Whiskey," she said. "Brand name."

"See that?" Bean asked Jesse. "She won't drink our stuff until maybe the seventh or eighth drink."

"Shut your face, Beanbag," she said, looking over at Jesse.

She opened her plastic imitation-alligator purse and pulled out her cigarette case. She crossed her legs as she nervously lit up, then leaned back with her eyes closed while she took a long, deep drag. When she opened her eyes she saw that her whiskey had arrived, and she lifted it quickly, exhaling the smoke through her nose into the glass as she poured it down her throat.

Then she resettled herself, recrossed her legs, and gave a slight smile.

"My name ain't Perkins, Bean," she said.

"Oh, that's right. Sorry ma'am."

He turned to Jesse. "Her divorce just come through two days ago, she's goin back to her old name."

"Oh."

"Little," she said stiffly. "I am Gloria Little from now on."

Jesse saw that she had a way of tossing her head slightly from side to side to make her hair fall just so.

"Drink this," Bean said to Jesse, sliding the beer to him.

"No thanks."

"Aw, come on. It won't bite you."

"No, Bean."

"I'll tell you one thing," he winked and leaned over and whispered. "If you drink it down, you'll be glad in a minute."

"I will?"

"You sho as hell will."

"All right, why is that?"

"Because them gals I was tellin you about are comin, and you want to be *ready*."

"Oh."

"I ain't kiddin. You gonna be nervous."

Jesse noticed that Gloria and Robert Elmer hadn't spoken to each other. They just sat close, stared out over the bar at the row of bottles and the cracked mirror, and drank their whiskies.

"I reckon I'll take my chances," Jesse said.

He had felt, this afternoon with Ren, that the anger and plotting against Paw was somebody else's dream, not really his at all. Now, slowly, the surge of meanness that made him feel like a Watersmith was coming back. It looks like I have to be this way, he thought, or they'll run me into the ground.

"Ain't Gloria fine lookin?" Bean asked him.

She glared at them.

"Uh, yeah."

"There's been many a bloody night in here over her," Bean said with pride.

"I'm not the only girl," Gloria said. "They's a lot of others."

"Oh, maybe," Bean said. "But I ain't never seen no *passions* riled up the way you can do it."

Somebody started the jukebox with one of Moe Bandy's cheating songs.

Now it was hard to hear and Bean leaned over into Jesse's face.

"See," he said, "Gloria is so *perfect* lookin. The beauty shop uses her for their ads and stuff. So they do her up for free. Gloria gets the full treatment four times a week."

"Good grief."

"She's somethin else. I'm tellin you. She's got the littlest waist in town, and the reddest lipstick. She orders that lipstick out of a catalogue from Paris, France, and she won't let nobody find out the name of it."

"And she likes Robert Elmer?"

"Hah! See, he come along one night when Gloria was fightin with her Frank. That's her ex. They was both drunk as skunks, and he was chasin her around this here bar."

"Whis*key!*" Gloria screamed, pounding her little fist. Then she resumed her statue-like pose.

"Man, she was upset. Old Robert Elmer tore into Frank and like to murdered him. He ain't been out of the hospital long."

"Is he the one who worked at the sawmill?"

"He's the one."

The lady bartender filled everyone's glasses.

Then, with nobody making him do it, just because he was thirsty and frustrated and dense blue smoke was burning his throat, Jesse lifted the glass of beer and took a cold swallow.

"All *right*," Bean yelled over the music.

"What the hell?" Jesse said.

"How'd that taste?"

"Kind of bitter, and salty."

"Try it again."

"Why not?"

He drank another swallow.

"At least it's wet," he said. He had always thought that alcohol would have a strong and immediate effect on him. But there only seemed to be a briny after-taste.

Bean finished the beer and his whiskey and called for more. Gloria and Robert Elmer were ready too. The place was jumping, with couples dancing around the jukebox, laughing and shouting over the wailing music. Only Gloria and his oldest brother sat staring ahead, just tapping their fingers and downing drinks. Gloria smoked all her cigarettes, crumpled up the pack, and threw it on the floor. Robert Elmer bought her two more.

Jesse began to enjoy the music.

He took a long swallow of the cool, fresh glass of beer.

"Man oh man," Bean said, "here I am drinkin with you. Never thought I'd see the day."

Jesse smiled grimly at him. He hadn't thought of it either. He looked around for a clock.

Where is Ren right now? What would she *think* of me? And how am I going to get back to her? Jesse saw himself putting the glass of beer down on the counter surface. He had taken another drink and not even noticed it. His mind was off a million miles away on Ren. He laughed at himself. It seemed suddenly that he could straighten his life out, if he just thought about it for a second.

"First thing I've got to do," he said out loud, "is find out about Paw."

"What?" Bean yelled.

"I've gotta find out about Paw tonight," Jesse yelled into his face over the jukebox.

"What do you want to know?"

"You can't tell me."

"You never know, little brother."

"Nobody knows but him."

"Knows *what?*"

"If he killed my mother."

"*Your* mother?"

"And yours."

"You don't need to worry about that."

"Why not?"

"Because it's over and done with, long time ago."

"No it isn't," Jesse said. "Maybe it's over with, but it sure isn't done with."

He drained the glass of beer. "Get me some more, Bean."

Bean laughed and turned on his barstool. He yelled for a round.

"Well, you can do whatcha want," Bean said, "but I think you oughta just forget it."

"Why?"

"Because—"

"Why, Bean?"

"Because she wasn't no damn good, that's why!"

"What?"

Bean seemed to sway back and forth in the fog of blue smoke. What was he talking about?

"She used to lay around all day. Claimed she was in her state, or some such thing. She wouldn't do no work, wouldn't even talk to us half the time."

"What was wrong with her?"

"Hell if I ever knew. Aunt May used to take care of her, used to say she was weak, 'just like a flower,' she'd say. 'You boys ought to be nice to her, leave her alone, because she's better than ten bushels of you all!' "

"Aunt May said that?"

"All the time. We wasn't near good enough to be around our own mother."

"That's what you remember?"

"You bet. Now *you* was a different horse altogether. You was everybody's pet."

Jesse noticed himself putting down the beer glass.

"Mama used to lay in a hammock between two trees. 'Bean, bring me tea, Bean, bring my fan.' She never quit. She never cooked a meal, never swept a floor."

"What floor?"

"We used to have an old frame house down on the road to the highway. It was a mess."

"What happened to it?"

Hank Williams was on the jukebox. Somebody turned it up louder.

"Huh?"

"I said, what happened to our house?"

"Oh! It burned. A nest of rattlesnakes was livin underneath it, and Paw got drunk one night and tried to burn em out!"

"That's when we moved up to the camp?"

"Yeah! And Mama got her hammock. The only one she'd let near that thing was you!"

"I don't remember a bit of that!"

"Well, you can bet me and Robert Elmer do! We used to hate you!"

The music was too loud to talk and they gave up.

Bean slid from his stool and staggered off to the bathroom.

Jesse raised the glass but it was empty. He took Bean's whiskey glass and gulped it in a single swallow. He didn't even feel it go down. He was drunk for the first time in his life and he didn't know it.

Jesse saw everything clearly now. He would find out that Paw had killed her, and he would do the old man in. It would be easy. Why had it seemed so hard before? Then he and Aunt May would live in town. He would learn things, and do things, and find a way to make Ren love him. It would all be easy. Ren. He had to get out of here now. Hitch a ride.

He looked up into the cracked mirror at the still, sad faces of Gloria and Robert Elmer. They just sat there and drank. What was wrong with them? Gloria tossed her silver hair from side to side. Through the haze of smoke waves she looked so lofty and calm. But every time she lit a cigarette or took a sip she seemed nervous. What a strange woman, Jesse thought.

Then a man was standing behind her and Robert Elmer.

She was turning around, Jesse was watching the back of her perfect silver hair in the mirror as he heard the man laughing insanely.

"You crazy bastards!" the man yelled.

"Oh, hell," Bean said, pulling Jesse's arm to get him out of the way.

"I got you a little message," the man yelled.

"Frank—" Gloria said.

"Shut up!" he snapped at her. "Listen! You Watersmiths, ever how many is in here of you? I got you a message from Mr. Evans himself."

Robert Elmer was standing now. He was bigger than Frank Perkins.

"He sent that crazy old daddy of yours up to a job today, to start on the sheriff's mother's timber."

Frank Perkins couldn't talk for laughing hysterically at them.

Bean was pulling Jesse toward the door.

"You know what the bastard did?"

"Get to it," Robert Elmer said.

"Oh, he wants me to get to it! You really want to know?" he screamed. "All right then, listen to this! Your daddy took the crew into the old woman's yard. Right in her yard! And they cut about thirty great big oak trees she had there!"

Frank was laughing so hard he couldn't talk.

"Well," he finally said, "the old woman had to be took to the hospital. Evans got ahold of your daddy and fired the sonofabitch, and fired you all too! You hear me? You *hear* me?"

Robert Elmer drew back his right arm to hit the man and Jesse saw it and he also saw it in the mirror. It would seem later to him that he could see that double arm any time he wanted to, just by closing his eyes. It was like slow motion. The arm came back, but then the pistol fired and there was blood all over Robert Elmer's shirt. Again and again and again, loud even over the blasting jukebox, and Gloria was screaming and Robert Elmer was sliding—again in slow motion—sliding to the floor as Frank Perkins kept shooting him.

Bean pulled Jesse through the open door and out to the pickup truck.

They raced down the highway and all the oncoming lights were doubled in Jesse's eyes.

Robert Elmer had to be dead.

They passed a screaming highway patrol car, blue lights whirling and siren rising, heading back toward The Water Hole.

Bean took the road up to town and Jesse couldn't look ahead as they started around the sharp curves. He was still in the bar, full of the poison blue smoke and his ears filled with the jukebox music. He could still see Robert Elmer and Gloria in that mirror, just as still as ceramic pieces in the gift shop.

Then he was sick all over the truck.

They reached town and Bean drove the length of it without slowing down. He never spoke until they were near the sawmill.

"I'm gonna drive this thing as far as I can," he said. "Past the mill and over by my tent in the edge of the woods."

"Okay."

"Then I'm gonna pack up all my stuff and head to camp."

"Right."

"You oughta come, too."

"I guess." Jesse knew he would never see Ren and Roxanne tonight. He couldn't go there drunk. He couldn't think clearly now.

They came to the sawmill and the headlights struck the big catalpa tree where he and Nathan ate lunch. It was lying over on the ground.

"Oh Lord," Bean said.

The truck skidded near it and they saw the fresh ragged stump, and the pile of bright sawdust. It had been cut down.

Bean stopped the truck and they stared at each other in the dark cab. Then they heard a terrible crash. Bean turned toward the mill and drove slowly. Half of the roof structure over the machinery had fallen down. Standing there before them, weaving back and forth with a chain saw in his hand, was Paw.

He was admiring his work.

They pulled up beside him and he whirled around.

"Bean!" he said. He laughed so hard that he dropped the saw. "Who else you got in there?"

"Jesse."

"Whatchall up to? Chasin poon?"

"Naw," Bean said, "we sho ain't. What the hell you doin?"

"Me?" Paw doubled up with his wild laughter. "I'm sawin down a sawmill!"

"My Lord."

"You boys stink."

"Aw, Jesse threw up."

"What's the matter with him?"

"He seen Robert Elmer get shot."

"He seen—" Paw stopped laughing. "He what?"

"We was down at The Water Hole, Paw. A feller come in and shot him."

"And you *left* him there?"

"He's full of holes, Paw. He's got to be dead."

"Lord. Who was it that shot him?"

"Perkins. That man he put in the hospital, Paw. Robert Elmer was sittin in there with his wife."

"I shoulda never let you boys come to town."

Paw stood there shaking his head.

In the distance there was the wail of a siren.

"Slide over," Paw said.

Bean started to but when he reached the mess he stopped. Paw opened the door and shoved him.

"Slide, I said!"

Paw revved up the engine and headed for the field's edge and the tents.

"This just can't be," he said.

PART III

Beside the River

Chapter 20

Jesse remembered stumbling through the dark woods.

There were briars across his face, roots catching his feet, snakes jerking away in the darkness.

He woke up in his old tent with a pounding headache, the air inside stifling hot.

Bean and Paw were sitting on the trailer steps. They waved tiredly at him and he barely returned it, then he walked away from them, down toward the creek.

It only carried about ten inches of water, but it was cool and he washed and drank from his cupped hands.

He sat down heavily in the deep shade of the trees and bushes, listening to the water cross a mound of gravel.

So that's what it looks like when somebody gets shot, he thought. Robert Elmer won't be back anymore. Never again. Never, never again Robert Elmer Watersmith. He shook his head slowly, eyes closed, and tried to take it in. Then he thought of Ren, waiting for him last night, and Roxanne and Nathan. At least it seemed Aunt May was gone, the only good thing, he told himself. Morning birds were singing in the leaves just like nothing had ever happened. But everything has changed, Jesse thought.

He grabbed his head and sat very still. The throbbing eased. Then he took another drink from the leafy mineral water, and started back to camp.

He didn't want to talk to them. When he came near the clearing he dropped back and circled, easing up behind the trailer.

He heard their voices, and he got down on his stomach and crawled slowly through the cool, powdery red dust beneath the trailer. He lay within a few feet of them, almost under the steps.

"We got to get Perkins," Bean said.

"Naw, we don't," Paw said. "It wasn't just him. It was all of them. You know that."

"Perkins pulled the trigger."

"Yeah. He couldn't just let Robert Elmer *be*. After all, that woman was divorced . . ."

"He shot him over and over."

"Shut up about that."

"We can't just let it go," Bean said.

"Well, we'll see. Wait a spell, see what happens."

"You afraid of the sheriff?"

"Hell no. He's afraid of me."

"Well, then what are we gonna do about it?"

"I hope we're gonna have some breakfast. Where you think May got to?"

"How can you talk about food, Paw?"

"Got to eat. Got to work, boy."

"What work?"

"Herrick says there's a big kill upriver. It ain't rained in a while, so it can't be the insecticides from the farms. Must be chemical plants dumping. I don't know."

"Them fish are on the way?"

"Already here."

"Oh."

"You take Jesse and go down to the grapevine banks. I'll start with the boat upriver and meet you at the big sandbar."

"All right."

"Yeah. We'll get these fish up and then I'll see what's going on in town."

"Think Perkins will get off?"

"Killin a Watersmith? Sure he will."

"Well, he won't get off from me."

"Now listen," Paw said. "I fixed the sheriff good when I cut his mother's trees. I fixed Evans, too. One thing at a time, though. Get it?"

"I reckon."

"You what?"

"Yes, sir. I can wait, too, I guess."

"That's my boy. Jesse been to the creek a long time."

"I'll pick him up on my way."

"Good."

They stood and Jesse lay in the shadow and watched their boots.

"Oh yeah," Paw said a little more lightly, "I got hold of that bobcat lure."

"That's good, I guess you can't wait for cool weather to try it out."

"Wait hell, Bean. I set three traps yesterday just to test it."

Bean laughed in his throat like Twaint.

"We'll find out about that stuff right quick."

"All right, Paw, see you at the sandbar."

"Sure will."

Jesse waited until both of them had been gone a few minutes. He lay motionless under the trailer with his eyes closed. He smelled the rank, lush vegetable swamp in the coming heat of the day, and the sour odor of the sagging trailer. He felt completely cut off from Ren and the town. It was almost as if Robert Elmer's death had shamed them in a new way. Especially since Paw attacked the mill. Jesse ground his teeth and felt his face tighten in the bitter, Watersmith lines. He killed Mama and it's like a curse on me and the whole family, Jesse thought.

Then he crawled out and walked inside. He crossed the dirty frayed purple rug into Paw's bedroom. Under the mattress he found the .22 revolver, an old single action, fully loaded. He looked for a box of shells but couldn't find one. He stuffed the .22 in his jeans, pulled his faded blue denim workshirt over it, and headed for the place they called the grapevine banks.

Bean was working the narrow channels that cut into the bank, places that held dead fish when the river floated them gently along this side.

Jesse watched him from the high bank above, then started down through the deep tangles of muscadine vines and Bean heard him.

"Hey!" he said. "How'd you know where I was? See Paw?"

"Naw. Just figured."

"Huh?"

Bean looked puzzled. "This is a good kill," he finally said. "Come help me."

Bean turned away from him and reached into the water. He pulled out a fish. It was a long alligator gar, hanging limp in his hand. "Nice one," he said.

"What about Robert Elmer?" Jesse said, his voice unsteady.

"Huh?"

"How can you just work like this?"

"Aw, Jesse. Paw says—"

"I don't care what Paw says. Don't tell me what Paw says."

"We can't get no revenge yet."

"Revenge?" You're going to find out what revenge means, Jesse thought.

"Yeah. We got to wait. Just like—"

"Shut up, Bean! Probably Robert Elmer deserved it. Maybe he didn't, but *we* don't know what was going on. I'm not talking revenge. I'm just saying he was your friend, wasn't he? More than mine. So how can you go right on with this mess, huh?"

"Aw, Jesse, Paw—"

"All right! Then just tell me this—"

Bean was already turned to his muddy channel. He

waded in and scooped up handfuls of the decaying
fish, scales sloughing off in his hands, bodies falling
apart into the burlap feed sack.

"Bean!"

"What?" he said, annoyed. "What now?"

"How can you sell this stuff?"

"What you mean now?"

"You know exactly what I mean. How can you let
people eat this?"

"Aw, I ain't doin that. We just sell this mess.
Somebody else feeds it." He chuckled.

"It's sick, Bean. I'm never touching it again."

"The hell you say."

"Goodbye, brother."

"What you mean?"

"You may not set eyes on me again. Hope you enjoy your life here with Paw."

There won't be any Paw for long, Jesse thought,
once I make my peace with Roxanne and have my
seance.

Jesse turned and started off.

"You listen to me!" Bean yelled.

Bean was standing in the muddy water.

"You ain't gettin out of nothin. There's just the
four of us left now. You hear me? Paw will get you
if you try to run. *You hear me?*"

As Jesse walked away through the woods he heard
his brother's voice, growing fainter and fainter.

"You think you're too good, don't you? You think
you're better than us! Well you ain't . . . you sho
ain't . . . you're a Watersmith, just like me . . .
Jesse!"

Jesse heard his voice rising, higher-pitched, hysterical and far away.

"You think we're just a bunch of rednecks. Well you ain't any better! You hear? You hear me?"

Then Jesse came to a stream falling over a bank. And the sound of the water erased Bean's voice.

He made his way around the camp and toward town. He stopped in the edge of a beanfield and ate a few shoots for strength, then headed for the high hill over the black section of town.

Jesse lay down here in the shade of an elm and waited. He held the revolver in his hands, turning it over and over, feeling the cold steel. Finally he laid it on the ground beside him and drifted off to sleep.

It was a fitfull nap, with dreams of fighting Robert Elmer, of his father yelling at him, coming for him. Aunt May was standing there, watching him, and Ren. They looked at each other slowly, shook their heads, and walked off together.

Jesse snapped awake and the sky was lavender. Bands of rose were smeared near the horizon, and the stars were clear overhead. He put the revolver in his belt, pulled his shirt out over it, and started down the hill toward Nathan's house.

Chapter 21

He stood on the porch, knocking on the screen. The fox slipped up and sniffed his knees.

Roxanne came to the door, recognized him, and fled to the back of the house. A moment later Nathan hurried up, opened the screen, and said, "Get in here, Jesse! Right quick!"

He turned and scuttled back toward the kitchen and Jesse followed.

They sat at the table.

"Now tell me first thing," Nathan said, "what is you doin down here?"

"What's the matter?" Jesse asked. "Is Roxanne scared of me?"

Nathan was twisting his hands together nervously.

"What happened to you last night?"

"I—"

"Never mind! We know! Don't think we don't!"

"Robert Elmer is dead."

"Yes, he dead. And that ain't all. Mr. Evans mad as a man can get, nearbout. And Miss Renly Anne, she come here all by herself, worried to death, and brought yo aunt with her."

"I couldn't help it, Nathan. My brothers came and got me."

"Came and got you?"

"Yes. At Miss Elmilly's. I couldn't get away."

Nathan looked at him and rubbed his bony chin.

"Aunt May was here?" Jesse asked.

"Uh huh. Look like the whole world know Roxanne's secret befo it over with."

"Was Aunt May all right?"

"She seemed to be. She come to Miss Robertson's place jus after you lef. Renly went over there and, later on, *both* them come back here. Young man, we waited for *hours* and *hours*."

Jesse looked at the toes of his boots. "They had me in the truck," he said.

"I don't doubt it," Nathan said in a resigned voice. "I don't doubt nothin."

"I've got to talk to Roxanne," Jesse said.

"That's what I was afraid you was gonna say."

"Please, Nathan."

"It ain't up to me," he said, rising. "It up to her."

Nathan left the room and he heard muffled voices arguing.

Then he came back and went to the stove without looking at Jesse.

"I'm makin me a little coffee," he said. "You want some?"

"Please."

"Uh huh. You eat?"

208

"Yes, I . . . had some beans."

Nathan looked carefully at him. "Out in the field?"

"Yeah."

"You don't look good," Nathan said. He tinked and clanged a few dishes and then presented Jesse with a plate of hot food. There were fresh peas cooked with fatback, cornbread, turnip greens, and a slice of ham.

"You lucky," Nathan said. "We ain't had this much to eat all summer. Thought our boy was comin home today, he been in jail a little while, but he didn't show up."

Jesse was too hungry to refuse and he tore into the plate of food.

"I'm sorry," he said, with a mouth full of peas.

"I'm sorry, too," Nathan said. "He was drinkin and fightin. Now Sheriff Riggins, he took a right smart interest in that."

Jesse ate and listened toward the other room. Roxanne was stirring.

Once Jesse finished his supper Nathan took the plate and handed him a cup of hot coffee. Then he stepped over to the bedroom door and called, "All right, Mother."

He placed two more cups of hot coffee on the table and sat down beside Jesse.

"I reckon we know what you want," he said.

Roxanne came into the room. She walked with a great sad dignity, not looking at Jesse, and took her seat. When she was settled in the small chair, she looked at him and spoke.

"I suppose you don't know nothin bout *halos*, do you?"

"Ma'am?"

Roxanne looked at Nathan.

"Everybody has a halo," she said. "It's a ring of light around your head."

"It's diff'ent colors," Nathan said. "Most folks can't see it."

"Can you?"

"No. No suh, I sho can't. But my wife can."

"The colors of them changes. A peaceful person, it's liable to be green or so. If you mad, it's gone turn red as blood."

"I see."

"One time I saw somebody didn't have *none* at all."

"You did?"

"One time, thas all. She died the next day."

"What is all this getting to?" Jesse asked.

"Yo halo is what. It's bout the color of a dark plum. Onc time it's purple and sad, the next minute it gets so red you could blow up an kill somebody."

He looked at her in alarm.

"I know you carryin a lot of trouble, Mr. Jesse, and I want to help. But I can't be no part of no killin."

"You *know* why I'm here?"

"I believe so."

"I want you to have a . . . I think they call it a seance."

"I know that."

"Have you heard anything from . . ."

"From Tanya?"

"Yes."

"Maybe, and maybe not. But look here. I didn't get my gift from no devil. It comes from Jesus Christ."

"I know that."

"*Do* you though?"

"You told me so."

"I told you lots of things. So did yo aunt, now, didn't she?"

"How do you know all this?" Jesse was angry.

"The good Lord don't *want* Roxanne to tell nothin if a person goin out and *misuse* it," Nathan said.

"All right," Jesse said. "I wouldn't blame you if you didn't talk to me anymore. But the reason I came here tonight is, I have decided to kill him. If you don't tell me what I need to know, I won't be back bothering you again. I'm gonna kill him anyway."

"If that the way yo heart has hardened why you come here at all?" Nathan said angrily.

"I'm satisfied he murdered Mama," Jesse said. "But I would *like* to be positive."

They were both watching him closely.

"Because . . ."

"Yes?" Nathan asked.

"I reckon I'm hoping you—I mean she, my mother—is going to tell me he *didn't* do it. I reckon that's it."

"And what you gone do then?" Roxanne asked.

"Well, I guess I'll just leave here. I'll try to get Aunt May far enough off that Paw won't ever hear of us again."

They sat there in silence for a while.

"I see," Nathan said at last. "And if we don't help you, you gonna do it anyway."

"I sure am."

Nathan and Roxanne looked at each other.

"I reckon you won't lie to me, either," Jesse said.

"I'd like to," Roxanne said.

"I know that."

"I don't know," Nathan said. "We damned if we does, and damned if we doesn't. If anybody knows you was here, then you go and kill a man, we liable to end up in the jailhouse."

Jesse realized Nathan was right. "I'm sorry. I shouldn't have come down here tonight. I'm going," he said. "I'm going right now."

But as he started to run through the back of the dark house Roxanne grabbed him by the wrist.

"Hush!" she said. They all waited, motionless for a long moment; Jesse felt her strength and felt his own desperate body ease a little.

"Hush, now," she said softly, as if nothing were wrong. "Nathan, this boy come here out of the *poison* inside him. It ain't like he was one of them KKKs. He come here with killin in his mind, now I can't say nothin good for him there. But I can feel this boy's soul tremblin like a bird. Befo he leave here tonight, I want to try to help him. You come in here," she said, pulling Jesse into the bedroom. "We gonna try to talk to yo mother!"

Roxanne sat on the sagging bed. Jesse stood until Nathan brought two chairs for them.

"No lights," Roxanne said. "And I want you to understand something, young man. I'm gonna try this thing because I want to help prevent you from throwin away yo life."

"Yo *foolish* life," Nathan added from the dark.

"I understand."

"All right. Now just sit still."

"Yes, ma'am."

"Shhhh."

They sat in the dark. A barking dog down the street was beginning to subside.

"Lord Jesus," Roxanne began, "we gather here to praise yo name. Hallelujah, Lord Jesus."

"Amen," Nathan said.

"We want to ask yo mercy on this young boy's struggle to escape the ways of his people," Roxanne said.

"He ain't no bad boy," Nathan added in a trance-like voice.

"He ain't got no mother, Lord," Roxanne said, "and he don't know everything about right from wrong."

"Amen," from Nathan.

"Lord Jesus, this boy has asked me to contact Miss Tanya, who is with thee we pray. If it be thy precious will, oh Jesus, let this poor boy talk to his mother tonight."

"Amen," Nathan said, "praise the Lord."

They sat still then, and waited.

It was hot in the room, and Jesse felt beads of sweat trickling down his face.

He put his hand on the revolver in his belt, and closed his eyes.

"Jesse?"

It was a husky woman's voice, coming from Roxanne.

"Jesse, are you listening?"

"Yes," he said scratchily. Goose pimples ran all over his neck and arms.

"This is your mother, honey."

"It is?"

"Poor boy. I thought someday, somehow, something would happen."

"You did?"

"Yes, honey. I always thought a new life was waiting for me. And you, too."

Jesse didn't say anything. Her voice was nothing like Roxanne's.

"But you have to make your own life, honey. I just waited for mine, and so did your Aunt May. And so do you, now, son. You are just like me. You wait and you wait. But that won't do."

"Did Paw kill you?"

There was silence.

"Did he?"

"I was trying to run away—I knew I could fall."

"Did he push you?"

"From the minute I married him."

"What do you mean?"

"I mean everybody chooses his life, and his death."

"Did he push you in, though?"

"Don't make yourself into a murderer, son."

"He killed you. Didn't he? Didn't he?"

There was silence.

"Didn't he? Tell me!"

They waited a long, hot moment. The dog barked down the street again.

"I've got to know!" Jesse cried.

"Stop it!" Nathan yelled. "Thas all of that! Stop it right now!"

Roxanne slumped over in the darkness onto the bed. The springs sang softly.

Nathan moved over Jesse's feet and turned on a dim light bulb.

Roxanne slowly rose up to a sitting position.

"Did she come?" Roxanne asked.

"Mo than come," Nathan said.

"*Lord* Jesus!"

Jesse rose so suddenly he knocked his chair over backwards.

He felt the pistol at his waist as he went out the front door, hearing Roxanne crying after him as he ran.

Chapter 22

Jesse ran up the dark streets and out into the woods. He had come so close. So close to hearing what he expected. Had she held back to prevent his becoming a killer? Or was this whole thing a crazy accident of some kind—some dream out of Roxanne's mind?

It's up to me after all, he thought. She's not going to come straight out and tell me. But I know he killed her, he must have. And there's nobody but me to make him pay.

Ren and her soft calming world seemed as if it never had existed, except as a hope, something he imagined but could never really find. The night of drinking and the shooting hung like a heavy curtain between her and Jesse now, as he walked angrily up through the trees, the sweat running down him in long rivers. The first thing he would do, the only thing he was sure about, was spring the new bobcat traps.

He moved through the blackberries and oaks and on into the cane around the beaver pond. Then, quietly, up around camp and toward the den. That was where Paw would have set them, he was sure. When he reached the sage hill he was exhausted. It was after midnight and the moon was down. He walked up into the thick sage and felt the ground. There were no prickly pear cacti, no rocks, and he carefully settled down on his back. Then he stretched from head to toe and closed his eyes. He tried to think things out clearly, but found he didn't want to. He didn't want to know what Ren was feeling, or to dwell on what he had already lost with her. His teeth ground together quietly when he remembered that it was Paw who had ruined her for him, even before he ever heard of her.

He woke in the rosy dawn.

He stood at the base of the hill, beside the thick woods, and jumped up and down, waving his arms. After a few minutes he was awake and he went to the old den entrance. There were no fresh tracks. Then he followed the trail from there to the north, around the edge of the swamp.

After half an hour he had found no traps. He cut down into the woods and circled back to the sage hill. He passed a well-used game trail, where he had always run traps. Paw had checked them with him at first.

He found the first one.

It was clumsily set, not deep enough, and crumbling dirt had exposed the pan and trigger.

Jesse set it off with a stick. Then he unwound the cable from its drag, and threw the trap as far as he could out into the woods.

That made him feel better. But it also let the bitterness toward Paw rise in him. He felt it like a warm liquid pouring into his body.

He followed the trail and found another trap.

Then he crossed plum and cane thickets into the woods again, and found the main animal trail running there. This one wound up beneath the water oak tree where he had watched the bobcat last spring. He followed it for a while, as the first bright rays of sunlight shot down through the thick leaves. The trees were deep summer green now, and some of the low weeds and bushes were faded from the heat. Everything was wet with dew, and his arms were gauzy from clearing the glistening spider webs out of his way.

He took a step but hung motionless in midair.

Ahead of him on the trail, just a few yards away, crouched low and perfectly still, was a bobcat.

Jesse's heart hammered in his throat.

The cat's ears went back flat, and the teeth showed suddenly for a second. There was a low sound of steam escaping.

Then he saw the trap. It was almost buried under the wildcat, and the chain and cable ran toward him, to a heavy short log which was the drag.

Tears came into Jesse's eyes. All the angry strength he had gathered for stealing Paw's traps was gone. It had happened. The thing he had dreaded for so long. He was just a little boy the last time they caught one. He remembered it now, stretched out dead in the camp. How it had filled him with astonishment . . .

His first thought was to somehow release the cat. Sometimes only their toes were caught in the iron jaws, and they would chew them off to escape. Once Jesse had found a single toe.

They could live just fine with a toe missing.

Maybe I could shoot off a toe, he thought stepping closer to look.

But the cat lept high in the air, fast as a blur he could hardly see, then was jerked down by the chain again. This time the front leg was exposed, broken at the main joint. A piece of white bone stuck out through the gray fur.

The cat's ears were dead flat, and the eyes were pure yellow liquid hatred.

Jesse had never seen anything so beautiful. So sleek, so smoothly brindled, colored to vanish like smoke in a reddish sage field, or a shadowy gray woods. There were highlights of all the woods colors, from white to charcoal and rust, and the cat was as still as a windless tree looking at him.

His eyes kept blurring from the tears.

He took out the revolver, cocked it, aimed at the head and pulled the trigger.

The report shocked him. The cat slammed to the ground, only a single hind leg hammering wildly into the dirt, throwing leaves behind.

It was dead.

He sobbed and sobbed, kneeling beside the bobcat, waiting for the jerking motion to stop. Blood ran in a bright trickle from the nose.

He reached down, trembling, and lifted the hind

leg. It was a female. Small. My cat, he thought. My female that I watched.

He wiped the tears from his face, and knelt down to take the trap off the broken leg. Then he sat beside the cat, too stunned to think. Minutes slipped by in the silent woods.

There was a crash in the brush behind him, but he was so much in shock that he was slow to turn around. Then another sound came, a limb being broken under a heavy foot. He turned.

Ren was sitting high up on Raffasha.

Jesse saw the sadness spreading over her face. Then she was staring back and forth from him to the cat, taking in the magical presence of that soft body even in death. Jesse saw all the questions in her eyes and the tears glistening on her cheeks, but as he opened his mouth she was already turning the reins harshly, Raffsha was turning, Ren's legs caught hold on her horse and as Jesse's scratchy voice escaped his throat Raffasha was already leaping, surprised and nervous and quick, already running away from him as he yelled, "Wait! Wait, please! Ren! Wait!" But she and the horse lept into a rush of kudzu and muscadine and leafy poplars, and the woods swallowed them up.

Jesse dropped back to his knees beside the bobcat. He pressed his hand over her heart. Warm fur, brindle and gray, spotted on the sides, striped on the back, and, when he rolled her gently over, snow white on her belly.

He searched in the long white hair and found the

teats. They were prolonged and wrinkled, but dry and tight. She probably had the kittens, up in her sage hill den, and had just gotten them weaned. I hope they know what they're doing, Jesse thought.

He stroked her head and neck, then down along her shoulders, as if she were asleep, or a pet. At least she wasn't feeling the pain of that leg anymore . . .

The bitterness came upon him in a wave. He looked at the great shafts of sunlight connecting the sky with the dark woods floor, the straight trunks of the trees, the leafy canopy crisscrossing above him. It was a holy place. She was a holy cat. Paw would never kill another one.

He stuck the revolver in his belt, and taking a front and back leg of the cat in each hand, lifted the body up over his head and down onto his shoulders. Then he rose, shifted, and felt the weight. She couldn't weigh more than fifteen pounds . . .

He knew the place he wanted.

With each step toward camp he hugged the cat closer, felt the steel of the revolver moving in his belt, and drew strength from the woods. Passing a deep bog covered with slime, he thought about the snakes in there, waiting and watching for a chance to hit a frog. The turtles, lying just beneath the surface with algae growing on their shells, listless as mudcakes in the sunshine, waiting for an insect or minnow. The whole woods seemed full of hunters, waiting, licking lips, finally striking in a flash of speed. Beetles destroying pine trees. Woodpeckers killing the beetles, one by one. Beavers forced to eat trees to keep their teeth the right length. Alligators lying like muddy logs to ambush beavers.

He was part of it.

He would get Paw, and he would never regret it, not once. And if Bean tried to interfere he would be next.

Jesse walked to the log in the swamp a hundred yards from camp, the place where he used to sit at night and call up owls.

He laid his cat down, very carefully, along the top of the log, so that her white belly fur showed toward camp. Paw would see her and focus all his attention there.

Then he walked along the trail toward camp, and eased into the briar thicket. There a young red oak grew, with a great oversized limb that arched above the trail. Jesse climbed the tree, and stretched himself along the limb.

He made sure he was comfortable, then tried his arm with the gun, up and down. Paw, coming along the trail from camp, would make a little turn, right where the brush was thick, and come just underneath him. He would see the cat. He would stop, staring at it, or slow down. By lowering the pistol Jesse could almost touch Paw's head.

Jesse was ready. The morning was still and cool. He would hear Paw in the brush. He would wait until the old man was right below him before lowering the gun. Other limbs full of lush shade drooped all around him, so he wouldn't be seen.

If he was not hungover, Bean would be on his

search for the rotten fish. There had been so many the day before that Jesse figured Paw and Bean would still be gathering them. And Bean would be out early. Only Paw, if he heard the shot, would come.

Jesse raised the pistol into the air and fired once. Then he held tightly to the tree and waited.

Paw would come and he would do it. And the world would be different. It already was. He couldn't think clearly. Only hang onto what he had to do. It was right. It would get rid of the worst man in the county. Poisoner. Killer. He remembered the deer, shot senselessly in the spring. And the voice in Roxanne's throat. He thought about Aunt May's face swollen shut, his own fear time after time. He looked back once at the cat, and hatred rose in him. There was a sound in the bushes. He cocked the gun. Footsteps. Deliberate and steady, coming quickly toward him. His mind wandered and he saw a picture of himself and Ren. He swallowed and his throat was dry. Footsteps louder. He had planned to wait and not lower the gun until Paw was right under him, but the brush was rattling, sticks were breaking underfoot, and he saw his own arm extended, the short barrel pointed to the spot where Paw's face would appear. He couldn't move his arm. It was just a stick, a limb, ready and stiff. All right then, he thought, all right. As soon as he steps into view, I'll aim. It's so close I won't miss.

Brush moved and the sound of steps reached the little turn. The trigger was a hard stone beneath his finger. He eased his skin off of it, so he wouldn't pull too quickly. It would be a quick jerk. No matter. He wouldn't miss. A form was in the leaves. He came down with great slow strength on the trigger, as slowly as he could, feeling the whole action as if it were a dream, and he saw the sights, the barrel, his arm, all lined up perfectly, motionless and steady, a fraction away from firing pressure, outlined against the worried face of his aunt.

He saw her bright dark eyes, the square sights aligned between them. He felt a flash of burning up the center of his extended arm, a streak of heat, and he felt the overpowering weight of that small trigger, pressing against his rigid finger.

He lifted his arm a few inches.

She saw him and stopped. His mouth was locked open, and his eyes were frozen wide. He held the cocked revolver straight out from him, pointing over her head.

She said nothing.

Chapter 23

Very slowly, Jesse was able to crook his elbow, and point the gun up in the air.

He laid a weak finger from his other hand in front of the hammer, and pulled the trigger. The hammer mashed softly, silently down. Then he found strength to lower the .22.

Aunt May stood looking up at him, her right hand raised to her breast, fluttering there helpless, then covering her mouth.

"Jesse," she whispered.

He felt himself draw into knots.

She looked at him with a long, astonished silence, until his legs swung down aimlessly and his arms lost their grip on the limb, and he fell hard into the dirt at her feet.

He curled into a ball, shaking without a sound, and tried to look up at her through his fingers over his face.

But she stepped over him.

She walked to the dead bobcat.

He couldn't look at her, just down at the dirt, at the revolver with its barrel packed where it had fallen.

"Get up," Aunt May said slowly.

He looked at her as she sat down on the log beside the cat.

She put her hand out to the cat's head, and started stroking very tenderly, barely touching her fur.

Jesse felt that he weighed a thousand pounds. He came over to her and sat down on the other side of the bobcat.

They sat still a long time, Aunt May petting the cat, arranging her whiskers and any long hairs that were turned the wrong way.

When Jesse was finally able to look at his aunt he saw her face turning red.

"You almost killed me," she said.

"I know."

"You *what?*" she fired back.

"I shouldn't have . . ."

"No! I should say not!"

Her face was redder than he had ever seen it.

"No you should *not!* What were you doing? Waiting for Twaint to ambush him?"

"Yes, ma'am."

"To kill your own father in cold blood?"

He looked down.

"Jesse!"

She crooked her head down and tried to see up under his face into his eyes.

"If anybody had asked me whether you could do

this, whether you had it *in* you to do this, I would have told them they were sick. Do you hear me?"

"Yes, ma'am."

"My poor boy," she said in a wilting voice. "Robert Elmer dead as he can be, and you tryin to turn yourself into a murderer."

"Oh, no, ma'am," he said suddenly. "I'm not a murderer."

She stared at him, angry and speechless.

"The devil you say!" she cried. "The very devil indeed! Waitin in a treetop and about to kill me and not a murderer? You're just as rotten as the dog that shot Robert Elmer."

"But you don't understand," Jesse said near tears, "he killed Mama."

"And Robert Elmer was sittin there with Gloria Perkins, too. So Frank or whatever his name is thought he had good reason. Jesse, is that *really* why you wanted to shoot Twaint?"

"Yes, ma'am."

"Well why *now*, of all times? I find out that poor boy is shot dead and I come up here huntin you, and right at that *minute* you make up your mind to do this?"

"Because I just found out for sure—"

"Found *what* for goodness' sake?"

"That he killed Mama, I *know* it now and—"

"Nonsense! Why do you say such a thing?"

"Roxanne had a seance, Aunt May, and Mama told me herself!"

"She most certainly did not! Nathan and Roxanne

came to me last night after you left there. They told
me what went on. And that voice didn't tell you a
thing."

"Please! Listen to me! Paw caught my cat, just to
test his stupid potion! Her leg was broken and I had
to kill her. Then Ren came. She must have thought
I *wanted* to do it—"

"Hush! Don't talk to me about cats! This is just
what I thought, Jesse—you're upset with your Paw
for the bobcat he caught, and for attacking Mr. Evans' mill, and Lord knows what all. Made you look
pretty bad with Miss Renly, didn't it?"

Jesse could hardly think. He was trying to retrace
his steps, to see if she was right.

"Now son, you had plenty reasons to be mad, no
doubt about that. But to *murder* the old buzzard?"

"But I thought I *ought* to do it."

"Why, Jesse?"

"So we could get away. You and me both."

Aunt May slapped her palms against her legs and
walked, exasperated, in a big circle.

"Now it was for *me? I'm* to blame?"

Jesse was trembling. "I'm sorry, Aunt May."

"Sorry?"

He looked at the ground. Things had turned upside down. He had felt justified in killing Paw. Now
it seemed he was just making up reasons to do it. I
was afraid to fight him like Bean and Robert Elmer,
he thought. So I was going to shoot him.

"Sorry won't get it," Aunt May said flatly. "The
real question is, what are you plannin now?"

"Ma'am?"

"Now! Now! When I'm gone and you're on your own again! Are you gonna climb back up in a tree with that gun?"

"No ma'am! I'm not!"

"Well, that's progress at least."

"I was wrong," he said. "I don't even know how I could have thought that way."

"Neither do I. Seems like the world's fallin down on me, Jesse. In one weekend's time I lost one boy I raised and near lost another one." She slumped down on the log beside the bobcat.

"It's all right now," he said.

"All right, is it?" she snapped back. "What's your next plan. I want to hear it."

"I may have been wrong to kill him, but I'm not putting up with him any more. And neither are you."

"Meanin?"

"Let's turn him in for the rotten fish."

"Put him in prison?"

"Yes, ma'am."

"What about the day he gets free?"

"We'll worry about that when we have to."

"We sure will."

"Aunt May, you don't have to have anything to do with it. I'll testify on my own."

"I'm afraid you'll have to, son. That strain would purely undo me."

"That's all right. Look, go into town and call the highway patrol, and tell them how to get to the grapevine banks. I'll meet them there this afternoon late."

"With Twaint?"

"If I can."

"Honey, I'm scared for you to—"

"No." He held up his hand. "I'm gonna do it. Just don't let Sheriff Riggins find out."

"Now there's a man who's ready and willin to shoot your Paw."

"I know it. Paw's got a lot on him."

"Yeah, and he ruined the sheriff's mother's place."

"Well, make sure the highway patrol doesn't tell him."

"All right."

"And one more thing, please."

"Sir?" She smiled very slightly at him.

"After you do that, would you try to find Ren, and tell her about the bobcat?"

"If my legs hold out."

She gave Jesse a long tight hug.

"I'll meet you at Miss Elmilly's late tonight," he said.

"Oh, Jesse." She hurried away without another look.

Chapter 24

Jesse walked slowly across the swamp with the bobcat over his shoulders. It was too early to go to the
river, and he headed for the tressel at Bluebottom
Creek. It was a long hot walk, but that was what he
wanted. He kept thinking of town, what it would be
like testifying against Paw and maybe Bean. He
would fix his father this way, then. Not kill him and
become like him, but stand up and denounce him in
court, and put him away to stop the poison fish business and all the rest. Paw could rot in his cell and
think · what his own son had done to him. And
maybe, he thought, there is even a space left for me
with Ren, with Mr. Evans.

He climbed up the slope with the beeches, their
roots embracing boulders, and he felt a flea on his
neck from the cat's fur.

But what am I? he said to himself. Just a thing that
changes with the wind. Here I was ready to kill Paw
and now I see that would be turning into him. He
saw his aunt's face against the pistol sights. He closed

his eyes. What if I had killed her? Then he remembered the gun. He had picked it up but its barrel was packed with dirt from the fall. He sat in the shade of a huge wrinkled-skin beech and cleaned it out with a stick. It flashed through his mind that he could still shoot his father. And then he was sick with himself: I'm so *tired* of being tempted, he thought, and changing my mind back and forth. Are other people this way? It seems like they're not—they know what's right and how much of it they want. I guess Aunt May must be something like this, too, waiting all these years, knowing she ought to leave. And Mama, too. Lying in the hammock and listening to birds. Wouldn't even talk to Robert Elmer and Bean. No wonder they got mean. And no wonder she jumped in the creek and drowned.

Jesse stopped. Suddenly he understood what Tanya meant, when she said she chose her death. She made that foolish run, maybe even timed it just right so that he'd catch her out on the beam over the flood, because she couldn't lie in that hammock and forget herself any longer.

And I would have chosen to be a killer, too. It didn't matter that Paw deserved it, because the world must be full of people who deserve it just as much. Like Robert Elmer, in the eyes of Frank Perkins. But Perkins chose to make himself a killer, that was just as important—more important—than killing his enemy.

Jesse reached the tunnel through the rock. He walked slowly along, listening to the whispering of the cold springs leaking down the mossy wall, and the clacking of his boots on the echoing stone. Then he saw the far side, bright and blinding at first, then just warm and still under the wide blue sky.

He wished he could skin the bobcat, to treasure and keep that beautiful fur all his life, to remember. It seemed that with her death, and his decision not to kill his father, something had ended. It needed to be marked somehow, and kept. But the fur would fall apart from the heat. So he climbed up to the top of the steep hill above the railroad with the cat. Here the ground was rocky and bare for a few feet, and he laid her gently down. At least, he thought, she will go back to the earth.

He sat down cross-legged beside her. The white dot in the center of each black ear-back, the spots of black in the long, thin white belly fur—she was beyond his power to describe and remember in every detail. And he wondered once again at the depth of his feeling, something beyond his words for her. He thought about what Aunt May told him, that his mother had a pet bobcat and he had played with it, and maybe that was why he cared about them so. But it wasn't enough. He'd had a vague idea that because the cats were so rare, and he was able to see them, that maybe he would someday see that other rarest thing in the world, his mother coming back. It was a silly idea, he saw now, but he was glad he had been able to hold onto it for a while.

No, there wasn't any explanation, he decided. It must be like Twaint killing deer, and so many other men, too. There must be something about why men love animals so much, even when all they can think of is killing them, that can't be really understood.

He stroked the bobcat's head and neck one last time, and got to his feet. He made his way down to the creekbed below, carrying only a few inches of clear water over the stones, and he took off his clothes and lay down a long time, washing and cooling himself. He wondered about his way of letting time pass, watching the high scuddling clouds and the treetops moving in a wind he couldn't feel below—and thinking, endlessly thinking, about his life—he wondered if that wasn't something he got from his mother, with her long slow days in the hammock between the poplars.

She seemed able to let whole years slip past, and Aunt May did, too—*all* of them—without really contacting the people in town, or, hardly, each other. Each one of them was as solitary as Twaint.

That's what I have to learn to break, he thought. How to know people and learn things and somehow be a lot more than I am, a lot more than I'd ever be in this swamp. Like Ren. Then Jesse thought there was another side to it, a love for these woods most people probably couldn't understand, that made his family's isolation, and the long slow days and nights filled with nothing but owls and crows and the whistling of quail and the splashing of beavers—made all this time important and good. It wasn't just being worthless lazy rednecks in the swamp. It looked that way from the outside, he thought, because of the things Paw did to people, and because town folks never are still long enough to feel what we feel.

So Jesse felt he had something special and important from his parents as well as his aunt, though it would be hard to describe and explain to anybody unless they already knew, from being in the woods themselves, what he was talking about.

He ate some blackberries, juicy and full of their sugar. Then he put his damp, dusty clothes back on, checked the revolver, and headed finally toward the grapevine banks.

The river made a long curve to the west, and the high inside bank of the turn was cut with channels like the teeth of a giant fish. The current tended to fill these backwater cavities with the dead fish and keep them trapped for a while. Thick masses of muscadine vines grew hanging from willows and oaks on top. Jesse knew it would take Bean half a day to work down the river's curve, and by then a new batch of fish would be washed in so that he could trudge upstream and start over. Paw would be cleaning out a dead lake, a big slough that was once the river's channel and was slower to fill. He should join Bean for the afternoon's haul.

Jesse hid in the tangles on the high bank and waited. Before him there was just the lazy calm river, its muddy surface hardly seeming to move until a log made its way down. He figured he would see them below, and he'd hear the state patrolmen coming above. Somehow he'd direct the officers to Paw and Bean. If he were lucky, he'd get away before the arrest . . .

When he heard a stick crack below he stopped and watched.

There was a little splashing, hidden in the tangles. Then Bean's head.

Jesse smiled.

Bean stood out clearly now and wiped the sweat from his brow. He squinted into the sun and looked tired, maybe confused. The gesture reminded Jesse of Bean when he was fun, playful, far from his father. Jesse thought how strange that he should be laying a trap for his brother—something he couldn't have imagined doing until now. But he could feel the hard lines of his angry Watersmith face forming. He was ready. You're going to get yours now, Bean.

He immediately felt sad again. His grudge against Bean was a weak one, not as strong as his affection for him. He hoped Bean would get separated from Paw in prison.

Then, from the corner of his eye, something on the river—Paw in the little aluminum boat. He was drifting down the edge, scooping up a fish now and then with the long-handled dip net. He disappeared into the overhanging vines.

They would meet in a minute. Then what? It must be near four. He had to hold them there at the curve in the river. Jesse heard a faint sound and strained his hearing: dogs. He watched and Bean's head was bobbing the way it did when he talked. Paw must be sitting in the boat, right in front of him.

What if they float downriver? Jesse stood up and called out, *"Bean?"*

There was a silence, then the quick answer.

"Here, Jesse!"

He climbed down as slowly as he could.

Finally he stood beside them on a little ledge of sand under the swirling vines. Bean held a short rope tied to the johnboat's bow.

"Where you been, boy?" Paw said angrily. Then, before Jesse could answer, he smiled and said gently, "I know you was upset about your brother."

It took the wind from him and he said, "Yes."

"Most pitiful thing I ever heard of. Shootin him down like that."

Jesse looked at them. They were muddy and streaked with sweat and a little sunburned. They sure do work at their life of crime, he thought.

"Got a lot of that mess?" Jesse asked.

"Oh yes," Paw said gravely, touching a full sack in the bottom of the boat.

"It stinks," Bean said.

"Goes fast in this heat," Paw said.

"Gonna sell it at the fish store?" Jesse asked.

"Sure am," Paw said, smiling boyishly.

Jesse reached under his shirt and pulled out the revolver. He cocked it and pointed it at Paw's stomach.

"No you ain't."

"Whoa now," Paw said softly, raising a palm. "What's this?"

"I am turning you in. Both of you."

"What?" Paw said to Bean. "What's this?" He started to laugh and Bean followed but it sounded forced.

"Paw," Jesse said.

The laughter stopped.

"You killed Mama, didn't you?"

"Now, Jesse," he said, closing his eyes and shaking his head and trying to smile. "Now you know—"

"Stop it."

They both looked at Jesse.

"Just stop it. You murdered her. And you know what the penalty for that is."

"Jesse?" Bean said, sounding very unsteady.

"Shut up, Bean. I set out to kill you earlier, Paw. I really did. But I decided that would just make me the same as you. Can you understand that? I didn't want to be like you." In the silence Jesse heard the dogs coming closer.

"Son," Paw said very softly, barely pointing with one crooked finger at the pistol. "Could you just uncock that thing? We don't want no accidents."

"No," he said. "I couldn't uncock it. Because I don't want anybody jumping at me."

He raised the barrel so it pointed at Paw's head.

"I decided to turn you in," he said, "and testify in a courtroom about these rotten fish. There's no other way, Paw."

"Oh no, son. Don't talk like this."

"We'll quit," Bean said. He sounded like he meant it.

"Sure," Paw said with a quick grin, cool as ever. "Why, we had no *idea* you felt so strong about it. We don't have to—"

"Stop it! I'm so sick of you lying to me, Paw. Can you imagine for one minute, for one second, how sick I am of that?"

Paw's eyes twitched back and forth. His mouth was working.

"I got to turn you in," Jesse said. "The highway patrol is on its way here, right now."

"You don't say!" Paw cried softly.

"I'm sorry Paw, and Bean."

"You ought to be!" Bean said.

"Lock us up!" Paw said. "Lock your old daddy up in the jail? You gonna do that to me?"

Jesse felt himself weaken for the first time.

"*You're* the ones ought to be sorry," Jesse said, "selling rotten fish to folks you never even met."

"Son," Paw said carefully, "let's make us a deal."

"No! Don't talk to me. I won't believe a thing you say. Just keep it to yourself."

Jesse pointed the barrel at Bean. "Get in the boat," he said.

Bean dropped his sack and hopped in. Jesse turned the gun on his father.

They heard the dogs louder.

"What's that?" Paw said.

"I don't know."

"Bloodhounds! Sheriff's bloodhounds! Listen."

"Can't be," Jesse said, but he strained into the sound. The sharp scent-striking bellows, driven from

big hound chests, were unmistakable. For a moment
Jesse thought he was listening to a winter deer drive.

"You said the state patrol, boy!"

"I know I did."

"I know them dogs! That's the sheriff! You know
what he'll do to us?"

"I—"

"You want your own brother killed?"

"No, I—"

"He might even shoot you, too, coverin his tracks.
They're on *your* tail!"

"I never called him," Jesse said. "I sent word *not* to
tell him!"

The dogs reached the edge of the banks and ran
back and forth, hunting a way down.

"Jesse," Paw begged, "Sheriff Riggins would kill
me before he'd ever arrest me. I got too much on
him. He'll kill your daddy this day, son."

He heard the brush again and hoofbeats. Then he
heard the dogs on top of of the bank.

He looked at his father and brother, cowering in
the little boat.

"Please, Jesse," Bean said.

The bloodhounds were falling through the grape-
vines.

"If I was to promise you—" Paw said.

"Stop it."

"Honest, Jesse," Bean said in a cracking voice. He
put his face down into his palms in his lap.

"Paw," Jesse said slowly. "Do you think you could
give up this fish business on your own?"

"Oh, yes! Jesse!"

"And leave off hitting Aunt May from this minute forward?"

"Oh, yes! But listen how close they are!"

"And what about trapping bobcats. Think you could quit that, just for me?"

"Anything, son, listen at them dogs!"

Jesse uncocked the pistol and kicked the boat out into the current.

The dogs were boiling in the vines.

"Watersmith? Watersmith!"

The boat silently followed the edge of the river.

As Paw and Bean looked back Jesse gave them a smile.

Chapter 25

Jesse lay in the oak shade beside Ren, listening to cicadas croaking loudly in the wind. The hot weather had been broken by a series of summer storms. His eyes were closed, and he heard above his thoughts, now and then, the swishing of the horses' tails against their flanks as they stood idly brushing off flies . . .

Facing the sheriff had not been hard. The puffing sweating man had found him high up the limbless trunk of a poplar, with the pack of bloodhounds snarling and baying below. When they were chained together and to a tree, Jesse climbed down and asked why they were trailing him. The sheriff didn't know whether to apologize or be furious. Jesse almost had him convinced it was a mistake, when he spotted Bean's burlap feed sack full of disintegrating gar, grendle, catfish, bass, buffalo, carp, perch and bream. He poured it out and stared, unbelieving, and finally held his big hand over his nose. Jesse told him the truth.

"You weren't supposed to come," he said. "I know you want to kill Paw."

The sheriff looked at Jesse, not knowing what to say.

"You can forget it," Jesse said. "I won't testify. You got no call to chase him."

"You already said," Riggins finally managed.

"Don't care."

The sheriff stared at him a long time. Finally he took the sack of fish as evidence. He left swearing it was enough to hunt Twaint down. And Jesse yelled after him that he had no case: he couldn't murder Paw on this account.

Aunt May was now living with Miss Elmilly. She had no idea why the highway patrol had called Riggins. They tried to pass that off as a minor slip.

"That was the deal," Jesse said. "My aunt told you so."

"You could be held yourself, young man."

"You could have gotten my father and brother shot down, too."

"You know they're guilty. You know somebody could die from those poison fish."

"I know the sheriff wants an excuse to kill them, too, and clean them off his record. This is not it. No sir."

Finally they had let him go.

And he felt good, standing up to them all, letting them know what he would and wouldn't do, and all of it based on the truth. The sheriff still claimed he would hunt Twaint down, and let the court worry about a case, but Jesse learned that he had lost his evidence to the heat and the tomcats behind the jailhouse.

Paw and Bean were lying mighty low, if they were still in the swamp. There was no telling what they would do in the future, but Jesse knew they'd never scare him the same way again, and he guessed he had established himself with his father: just as Robert Elmer and Bean had done, in their own ways, before him . . .

"Jesse?"

"Huh?"

"You asleep?"

"Just thinking."

"We better water the horses before long."

"Uh huh."

"You know what Miss Elmilly told my daddy?"

"What?"

"She thinks you could go to the high school this fall, if they'll put you in different classes, different grades, at the same time."

His eyes opened.

"I don't know that I want that."

"Who cares what you want?" Ren laughed. "It would make school more interesting for *me*."

"I wouldn't know anybody."

"Until you went, of course."

He closed his eyes again and stretched on the grass.

"You said you wanted to learn things," she said, "break out of your, uh, circle—" he opened one eye toward her.

"Yes."

"Well, I think you should do it."

"Okay."

"Just like that? You'll do it?"

"If I *can*. If I can do the work."

"Oh *good*," Ren said.

They were still for a while longer; the air carried a distant hum from a harvester cutting hay.

"I sure am glad," she said slowly, "you didn't shoot your aunt."

He rose on his elbows, blinking.

"You know about that?"

"She told me not to tell you."

"Oh?"

"I was so surprised, Jesse. You know, even though you told me your plans, I didn't want to believe it."

"You didn't think I could do it?"

"Well, anybody could if they were pushed enough, I guess. But I didn't think you could plot it out so. . ."

". . . Cold bloodedly."

"Yes."

"I almost did, though, And here's the thing I keep thinking: it was so much luck that kept me from it. Luck."

"You seem disappointed in that."

"I am. It makes me feel weak."

"You *were* lucky."

They sat side by side, arms wrapped around knees. The horses' tails slowly fanned.

"But you *didn't* pull the trigger, did you?"

"No."

"And maybe you wouldn't have, even if—"

"It had been him?"

"Yes."

"Why do you think that?"

"Well, later on, at the river, didn't you *save* them . . ."

"But that was after Aunt May. After what almost happened to her."

"Maybe. But even if you did have a piece of good

luck there," Ren said smiling, "don't you think you were about due for some?"

He laughed slightly.

They walked the horses slowly through the oak grove. When they came to the fields near town they stopped a moment and looked out of their shade across the bright expanse of soybeans and hay. It was a fine private moment and Jesse wanted to hold onto it but Ren smiled and led the way out into the light.

J   Wallin, Luke
Wal   The redneck poacher's son.

	DATE DUE		
	MAR 2 4 2000		

Deaccessioned